THE★SHOW

THE★SHOW

Loose Lips

by Jordan Cooke

Grosset & Dunlap

GROSSET & DUNLAP
Published by the Penguin Group
Penguin Group (USA) Inc., 375 Hudson Street, New York, New York 10014, USA
Penguin Group (Canada), 90 Eglinton Avenue East, Suite 700, Toronto, Ontario
M4P 2Y3, Canada (a division of Pearson Penguin Canada Inc.)
Penguin Books Ltd., 80 Strand, London WC2R 0RL, England
Penguin Group Ireland, 25 St. Stephen's Green, Dublin 2, Ireland
(a division of Penguin Books Ltd.)
Penguin Group (Australia), 250 Camberwell Road, Camberwell, Victoria 3124, Australia
(a division of Pearson Australia Group Pty. Ltd.)
Penguin Books India Pvt. Ltd., 11 Community Centre, Panchsheel Park,
New Delhi—110 017, India
Penguin Group (NZ), 67 Apollo Drive, Rosedale, North Shore 0632, New Zealand
(a division of Pearson New Zealand Ltd.)
Penguin Books (South Africa) (Pty.) Ltd., 24 Sturdee Avenue,
Rosebank, Johannesburg 2196, South Africa

Penguin Books Ltd., Registered Offices: 80 Strand, London WC2R 0RL, England

Cover designed by Ching N. Chan.
Front cover image © 20 Something/Stockbyte Photography/Veer Inc.
Back cover image © Anatoly Tiplyashin/iStockphoto/iStock International Inc.

Copyright © 2008 by Grosset & Dunlap. All rights reserved. Published by Grosset &
Dunlap, a division of Penguin Young Readers Group, 345 Hudson Street,
New York, New York 10014. GROSSET & DUNLAP is a trademark of
Penguin Group (USA) Inc. Printed in the U.S.A.

Library of Congress Control Number: 2007049043

ISBN 978-0-448-44687-5   10 9 8 7 6 5 4 3 2 1

The 'Bu \ thə bōo\

1: popular nickname for California's
   legendary Malibu Beach, as in Mali*bu*.
2: the hottest teen beach drama ever to hit
   TV land (see inside for actual script pages).
3: a complete and utter freak show.

One

Somewhere in the Woods of Holly—Mid-August, Sunday, 3:05 P.M.

;The Bu-Hoo

'Bu, babies . . .

My children . . .

The ones wandering in the darkness . . .

The ones who look to me for answers . . .

Answers to life's questions!

GUESS WHAT? I'M BAAAAAACK!

MBK missed you, kiddies. Dincha miss me? For those of you just tuning in to 'Bu-hoo Land, MBK stands for Malibu Barbie *and* Malibu Ken. But all kinda mashed together so you don't know which I am! Pretty clever, huh? MBK thinks so.

So anyways, I went down to the Baja Peninsula for a few weeks and lost track of time. Sorry to leave you kiddies in the lurch while I was gone. I did learn one important thing down there I thought you should know: Don't drink the water!

All regurgitation aside, I see from the spike in 'Bu-hoo traffic that a whole heap more peeps are currently tuning in to this here blog. *'Bu-newbies* I'll call them. *Muy interesting* as they say below the border. Maybe these *'Bu-newbies* are tuning in because *The 'Bu*—that brand-new, bikini-licious teen drama—is about to make its debut on the UBC television network . . .

Well, holla, *'Bu*-newbies! You've come to
the right blog. *The 'Bu* is going to set your
television on fire with bangin' bods and
poppin' story lines. Not to mention all the
whacked stuff the zegxy, zegxy cast gets up
to when they ain't on the set! Lordy, lordy,
does the dirt fly! What's that you say? You've
missed out on all the gossip so far? You feel
all stoopid because you're coming late to the
party? Aww, poor *'Bu*-newbies.

Just to show you how good MBK is, I'll take
a moment to get y'all up to speed . . . .

Once upon a time there was an over-hyped
music video director who had an idea for
a TV show called *The 'Bu*. He was only
twenty-six, but he already had a gigunda
see-through house in the Hollywood Hills with
its very own walk-in tanning salon (seating for
twelve). He also had a totally fake-o name
(Max Marx!) and a voice with two levels:
whispery when low and girly when high.
Truth is, this dude was a no-talent Prada
mannequin with salsa verde where his brains

should be. We call him M2.

So M2 gets really lucky and pulls together a cast full o' hotties. Not only does he snag the luscious and lickable Anushka Peters (a standout on last season's *Suburban Magic*), he also nabs Tanya Ventura, teen cover-girl sensation and good Catholic girl (who has a promise to Jesus to keep her legs crossed until marriage).

Hot stuff, right? Of course, Anushka never met a bottle of champagne she didn't like, and there isn't room in Tanya's tiny brain for two thoughts that make sense together, but boy do both of them look good wet!

SEE LINK: <u>MOIST CELEBS</u>

M2 hired some smoking actor dudes for this little show, too. Rocco DiTullio, the brooding Italian Stallion from the legendary filmmaking Bellucci clan, and the delicious but mentally compromised SoCal love monkey Trent Owen Michaels (the cable series *Emo Surfer* shot him straight to the middle).

Trent had it bad for Tanya, and for a short time they made the prettiest empty-headed couple the Malibu coast had ever seen. Then . . . tragedy struck. Okay, not really tragedy. Tanya just got a little caught up in the excitement of Hollyweird and decided maybe she wanted to play the field. IS THAT SO WRONG??? So maybe this golden couple ain't exactly *ovah*, but they certainly won't be making any sex tapes anytime soon. :)

CUE MUSIC: "Since U Been Gone"

Rocco, on the other hand, had a love life that was going *nowheres*. He was too busy reading books by dead Russians and hanging out with his hyperactive, sunken-chested sidekick Jonathan Bader (aka JB) (aka Master Bader). JB was addicted to all kinds of naughty online behavior—and we *applaud* him for that!

Great cast, yes? Gorgeous, talented—and totally mental. Seems like M2 should have been able to knock *The 'Bu* straight out of the ballpark, yes?

Well, NOT EXACTLY.

Executive producer Michael Rothstein (we call him Goth Roth) rode M2's Prada-clad butt the entire time *The 'Bu* pilot was filming. Goth was spending millions and M2 wasn't delivering. That's because M2 was too busy contemplating his photo-ready cuticles to actually do any *real* directing.

Thank God Corliss "Clueless" Meyers rode into town in her trusty Mazda rental! A fashion-challenged misfit with occasional premonitions and kooky psychological insights, Clueless had come all the way from some state that begins in a vowel to move in with her uncle Ross, an award-winning screenwriter. Uncle Ross promptly got Clueless an internship on *The 'Bu*, which was about to begin filming its very first episode. She had no idea she was there to save the day, but guess what happened next, kiddies? Clueless became M2's assistant and goaded him on to complete the kickin' pilot. The kickin' pilot was then delivered to Goth Roth on a silver platter. Goth Roth loved the kickin' pilot so much he ordered a full season of kickin' episodes and our cast went on summer hiatus so the writers could write 'em. Actually, make that *writer*. Poor Petey Newsome, prodigy from Harvard, was the only writer left standing after M2 fired all the others. So, Petey spent the summer hard at work—but also pining over his two muses— Clueless Meyers and Anushka "Champagne Breath" Peters. So sad. Both these chickies put this raccoon-eyed dude squarely in their "ick" columns.

And speaking of starlets who need breath mints, no one's seen Little Miss Peters in, like, forever! M2 totally canned her million dollar bootay after she set Malibu Canyon on fire with a ciggy butt. OOPS! That little stunt cost the UBC network millions in insurance premiums—and just about sunk Anushka P.'s career. Of course, she's all lawyered up and expects to get a pile of wrongful termination cabbage, but still, that's gotta hurt!

Official word from her publicist's office is that the vertically challenged Miss Peters has given up the business of show. Can you believe?! Is she *really* at Pomona Tech studying hard, learning the ins and outs of *psychology*, like they want us to believe? Or is she out on the town and delivering the drama???

You know which one we're voting for! This girl is *bananas*—and one of the primo reasons MBK lives!! So keep checking in, kiddies. Newbies or oldbies, you are all *'Bu*-babies to me.

Yours in fa-*'Bu*-lousness,
MBK

The Kodak Theater—Hollywood Boulevard—A Few Hours Later

Hundreds of cameras were aimed at Anushka, shooting off a gazillion watts of light. Paparazzi screamed her name—Anushka! Anushka!—and she obliged them by looking seductively at each, flicking her gorgeous buckwheat mane this way and that, flashing her lunar blue eyes and curling her ripe, red mouth into a sly smile.

"Pretty much as it should be, don't you think, Jeebs?" Anushka elbowed JB, who was at her side.

"Ow, Anush, I think you just broke a rib."

"Ha! I might elbow like a wrestler, but I look like a goddess, right?"

She sure did. And she'd worked for hours to make sure. This was the Teen Choice Awards and *everyone* was there: Hugh Dancy, Hilary Duff, America Ferrera—even Paris and her pocket pooch.

Anushka knew the otherworldly glamour of these stars meant she had to get her gorgeous on if she wanted some PR play. She'd chosen a devastating sleeveless, silk, sky blue Alexander McQueen dress that hung off her like she was a goddess. The dress was slit up to her thigh and sliced down to her belly button. There was as much Anushka showing as there was McQueen.

"Anush, jeez, there sure is a lot of you hanging out! Not that I'm *complaining*."

"Cool down, Jeebs, you've got a whole night ahead of you to stare at these boobers."

"Right—pace myself."

"You look pretty smokin' yourself, Jeebs. I had no idea you cleaned up so well."

He sure did. Turned out head to toe in Fendi, JB was looking classy and mature. He'd even removed his retainer for the evening's festivities. "Thanks, m'lady. I took out the food trap and everything. But what about that dude?" JB pointed to the stoned surfer on Anushka's *other arm*.

"You mean Tyler?"

Tyler was weaving back and forth, his eyes barely open. Wearing a Ted Baker seersucker suit and Havana Joe slides, Tyler was totally rumpled, totally adorable, and totally out of it. Anushka elbowed Tyler but it barely registered. "Looks like Tyler needs a latte . . ."

"Wha?" said Tyler, suddenly stirring to life.

"Hey, Ty," said Anushka, "step lively. You're gonna end up in the back pages of *Us Weekly* looking like you just crawled out from under Amy Winehouse."

"Wha?" said Tyler.

"Oh, forget it." Anushka meant it; there were too many photographers to wave at. And too many stars to blow kisses at.

"Where did you pick him up, anyway?" asked JB. "Stoned Surfers R Us?"

"Listen, JB, save the smartass talk for your boyfriend, Rocco."

"Ouch! I guess Rocs and me *are* a little homo sometimes."

"*Sometimes?* You two are so close you make the Wilson brothers look like distant cousins." Anushka waved to her fans as she continued her explanation. "Look, I *knew* I had to make a good impression tonight. That's why I brought someone hot—like Tyler—and someone totally legit and boring like you." Anushka kept waving and smiling while talking to JB out of the side of her mouth.

"You flatter me. And have you ever considered a career in ventriloquism?"

"Whatevs."

Just then, Tyler leaned into Anushka and whispered in her ear, "I need to drain the dragon."

Anushka talked to JB out of the side of her mouth again. "Need a favor. Can you take Tyler to the little surfer's room, Jeebs? He says he needs to tinkle." Anushka kept waving. JB sighed. A reporter approached with a helmet of blond hair, a way-too-short skirt, and a look of manic happiness.

"Anushka!" the reporter called. "It's *Access Hollywood*. Can we say hello?"

"*Of course!*" said Anushka, making a beeline for the reporter. "I *looooove Access Hollywood*."

"Wait!" said JB, grabbing Anushka's elbow. "I'll take Tyler to the little surfer's room but *don't* say anything you'll regret, okay?"

"Whatevs," said Anushka out of the side of her mouth. "Now get a move on before Tyler takes a whiz on Melissa Rivers." She nodded in the direction of Tyler, who was tilting perilously close to Melissa Rivers.

As JB steered Tyler to the nearest porta potty, Anushka approached the reporter. "Alexander McQueen," Anushka said before the reporter had a chance to ask about her dress.

"You look *gorgeous*, Anushka. Slim and tan and

oh-so-healthy!" The crowd cheered. Anushka waved and smiled. "Life after *The 'Bu* obviously agrees with you."

"Thank you," Anushka said with perfectly perfected fake humility.

"And I understand you're going to school?"

"That's right," Anushka said in the strange British diction she sometimes used when being interviewed. "I'm studying psychology and I love it! Show business is fine for *some* people. But what I've always been most interested in is a life of the mind." She then subtly tipped forward to better show off her cleavage.

"That is *so* admirable, Anushka. But I'm sure your fans want to know if there's any chance you'll be joining *The 'Bu* later in the season? Word has it that it's going to be the biggest show on fall TV! Or has that particular bridge been burned? There was a lot of talk about your behavior on the set . . ."

Anushka pursed her lips into a tight smile. She wanted to pull the reporter's blond weave out of her scalp and smash it into her too-tan face, but she swallowed her rage like a huge wad of gum. "Oh, *no, no, no*," she said. "I was only meant to be a very special guest star in the pilot—for reasons you'll see when it finally airs—so returning to *The 'Bu* is really out of the question."

"But there are rumors—"

"Please," Anushka said, shaking her head with perfectly perfected fake demureness. "I've decided at this point in my life not to pay attention to rumors. I've also decided that I do not want to be a part of any more . . . *toxic environments*."

"That's quite a thing to say," said the reporter, almost

salivating. "Are you implying there's tension on the set of *The 'Bu*?"

"Not at all," said Anushka with an exquisitely fake innocence. "What might seem toxic to *me* might be perfectly acceptable to other people. People less experienced, let's say." Anushka knew she was being provocative, but she couldn't help herself—or hold her tongue. "Haven't you been to TheBuhoo.com? It's all there in black-and-white."

"What's TheBuhoo.com?" said the reporter, smiling crazily. "Do tell!"

"TheBuhoo.com is a blog," Anushka continued in her clipped, fake accent. "It's all about *The 'Bu*—but a behind-the-scenes account, if you get my meaning."

"Wowzer! That sounds exciting. TheBuhoo.com, everybody!" the reporter shouted to the crowd. "Check it out now!"

The crowd cheered and a sea of cell phones, BlackBerrys, and iPhones were raised in unison. Anushka's eyes glowed as she relished her Teflon star power.

Holmby Hills, Uncle Ross's Home Theater—Continuous

"*Noooo!*" shouted Corliss at the larger-than-life image of Anushka being broadcast live on Uncle Ross's ginormous flat-screen TV.

"Oh, dear," said Uncle Ross from the bar across the room. "What is that adorable little vixen up to now?"

"Only digging herself into a bigger hole than ever—and creating trouble for me in the process!" Corliss thought fast. She dug into her pocket for her phone and quickly called

Anushka. To her astonishment, she heard Anushka's phone ringing on TV.

"This is *so* embarrassing," said Anushka to the reporter as she looked in her Julie K microsuede handbag and checked the number. "Oh, look! It's my girlfriend Corliss Meyers. She works on *The 'Bu!*" She answered her phone as the reporter looked on in amazement. "Cor! I'm on the red carpet! Do you want to give a shout-out to *Access Hollywood*?"

"No! I *don't* want to give a shout-out to *Access Hollywood*, Anushka, and *stop* talking about the blog for God's sake! Okay?"

"Love you, too!" said Anushka, waving from the TV.

"Oh, dear," said Uncle Ross, passing a bottle of vermouth over his second martini. "Little Miss Peters can't keep her pretty trap shut, can she?"

Corliss turned the TV off. "I can't watch any more."

"You're as white as a sheet, Corliss. Even that orange spray tan you got in the Valley yesterday seems to have worn off."

"I just can't believe Anushka would do that! She knows *I'm* the one who's going to have to deal with Max tomorrow. Why do I still have to pick up her poop?"

"Corliss, never say 'poop.' And worry not about Max. You seem to have him wrapped around your rather ineptly manicured little finger."

Corliss blushed a little and couldn't help smiling. "It's true, Uncle Ross. Ever since he hired me as a real assistant, it's like anything I say goes! Whenever we're working with Petey on the new scripts, Max turns to me and says, 'What do you think, Corliss?' Can you believe it? It's like I have all this power after a lifetime of *zilch power*."

"Just don't let it go to your pretty little head, Corliss. You know I can't abide uppity people under the age of thirty."

"Don't worry, Uncle Ross. I'm still totally myself. Underneath my recently refurbished exterior still lives Corliss Meyers, homely denizen of Indiana-no-place. I just better text Max and give him the heads-up about Anushka—if he isn't getting a gajillion calls about it already."

As Uncle Ross watched Corliss text Max, he sighed. "Corliss, you've become such a savvy television professional. Are you really sure you want to give it all up to go to college?"

"We've been through this a million times—yes! I worked all through high school to get into a good college, and in just over two weeks I'll be sitting in a classroom at Columbia University learning about mental illness. How cool is that?"

"Oh, Corliss," said Uncle Ross, clutching the piping of his day pajamas, ". . . classrooms . . . mental illness . . . are you sure that's what you want? It all sounds so *grotesque*." He shuddered a little.

"It's what I've wanted my whole entire life—to get inside the workings of people's minds so that I can help them."

Uncle Ross made a strange sound like he was throwing up in his mouth. "Corliss, my darling, it's all well and good to want to, um, *help people* . . ." He made the strange sound again. "But I think you're crazy to leave Los

Angeles now. You've made such inroads here! And besides, many successful people *never* went to college. Visionaries like . . . like . . ."

Corliss could tell he was having trouble coming up with some names. "Yes . . . ?"

"Well, like Paris Hilton. And . . . and . . . Britney Spears."

"Those are terrible role models, Uncle Ross. They keep forgetting their panties."

"Corliss, please, you know the word 'panties' sends me round the bend."

"Sorry. But besides, Paris and Britney are in show business. I'm going to be a psychiatrist—a serious profession. I need a degree. I'm totally going to miss working on *The 'Bu*—and, of course, living here with you." She hugged her uncle hard to make sure he knew just how much.

"I'll miss you, too, dear, but these day pajamas are Como silk, and if anyone so much as exhales on them they pucker like an elephant's behind." Corliss let go. "Let's make the best of our remaining time together, Corliss. You want to get in the Bentley and drive into Brentwood for some Pinkberry?"

"I'd love to, Uncle Ross, but I think I'll pass. I'm going to need a good night's sleep under my belt to deal with Max and this Anushka mess tomorrow morning."

"Oh well," said Uncle Ross, sighing heavily and passing the vermouth bottle over his third martini. "I guess I'll just turn the TV back on and see what that incorrigible Tyra Banks is up to."

Corliss gave Uncle Ross a big kiss—making sure to

go nowhere near his pajamas—and then dashed upstairs, yelping as she went. "Just think! In two weeks I won't have to deal with any more Hollyweirdness! Woo-hoo!"

Two

The 'Bu Production Office, Zuma Beach—9:12 A.M., the Next Morning

Max Marx groaned at the carnage splayed across his desk. *The Post, the Daily News, the L.A. Times.* Each newspaper cover showed Anushka in her devastating Alexander McQueen at the Kodak Theater the night before. In every image her big red mouth was open about a foot wide. "Are there more of these?"

"Uh-huh," said Corliss, standing on the other side of his desk. "These are just the greatest hits selection." She laughed weakly. "And there's more sucko news, I'm afraid. Apparently, The 'Bu-hoo had another big spike in readership—about ten thousand more people as of this morning. At least that's what the blog claims. Who knows what to believe?"

Max took a big breath and reached for his prescription migraine medication. He popped a few and started crunching them.

"Don't you want some water with those?" Corliss said, wincing.

"No, thank you, Corliss. I find the pulverizing sound my

jaw makes when I do this to be oddly comforting."

"Look, Max, you and I both know Anushka can't help herself," said Corliss. "She gets a little attention and those gums start flapping and—"

"Corliss—"

"Before you say anything more, Max, just know that both my witchy side and my psychologically intuitive side recognize Anushka's latest stunt as a grab for attention and nothing more."

"That may be. But I just got off the phone with Michael Rothstein, our esteemed producer. You might remember his vaguely insane wife, Mingmei?"

"How could I forget? She accused me of being Anushka's poorly dressed lesbian assistant."

"You're hardly poorly dressed, Corliss."

"And I'm hardly a lesbian assistant! I mean, I am an *assistant*, and I do like Ellen DeGeneres's talk show, and sometimes I watch *The L Word*, but that doesn't mean I want to lip-lock the ladies."

Max wrote the phrase "lip-lock the ladies" in his BlackBerry. "Your latent lesbian tendencies aside, Mingmei told Michael Rothstein that she had a terrible dream that Anushka Peters brought down *The 'Bu*! And Michael Rothstein doesn't want *anyone* to bring down *The 'Bu*. In fact, he will bring down anyone who wants to bring down *The 'Bu*. That includes your friend Anushka."

"She *is* my friend, Max. Which is why I know she would never, ever—"

"Corliss!" He put his hand up to silence her. "Please cease."

Corliss looked hurt. "Max, you haven't said 'please cease' in, like, two months . . . Is something wrong? I mean, like, are you and I having a problem?"

Max slid down into his chair. He felt awful. Corliss *had* been exceptionally helpful to him the past two months, making excellent suggestions about the new scripts Petey had been busy working on, and generally offering her patented strange but productive insight.

"I'm sorry, Corliss. It's just that the actors will be coming back to start filming the second episode and the thing is . . . the thing is . . ." Max looked out the window of the office to the beach outside. He struggled with revealing his innermost insecurities. "Well, what if I *am* just a 'no-talent Prada mannequin with salsa verde where my brains should be'?"

"What?! Who said that?"

"I don't know who said that, Corliss, because whoever said it is hiding behind the moniker MBK!" Max heard his voice get girly, and he made sure to modulate it down before he proceeded. "I read that despicable quote on The 'Bu-hoo yesterday and I haven't been able to get it out of my head. Oh, I'm not worried about the blog itself, really. Or even all the people reading it. Any publicity is good publicity as far as I'm concerned. What I am worried about is *my reputation*."

"I see," said Corliss.

Max thought he saw Corliss roll her eyes, but then he became distracted by the sight of his worried face in the enormous mirror that hung on the wall opposite his desk. He'd installed it so he could look at himself while talking on the phone to boring people. He stared deeply at his angular visage and thought really hard about being lacerated publicly online. But mostly, he admired his hair. It was thick and chopped and glistening. He knew having such hair gave him real authority. *Why should I be worried about my reputation when I have hair that can do this?* he thought. He resolved to put The 'Bu-hoo and all the trouble it was causing out of his mind.

"All right," he said to his reflection. "Buck up, Max Marx. Tomorrow you begin filming the second episode of *The 'Bu.* All your focus should be on *that* and *not* on your hair."

"Your hair?" said Corliss, waving a little to remind Max that she was still in the room.

"I mean *my reputation*," Max corrected. "You always know what's important, Corliss. And really, you need to forget about this 'Bu-hoo business. The UBC will sic their lawyers on this MBK person and in a few weeks that blog will be ancient history. At that point, you and I will be able to concentrate on more important 'Bu-related things."

"But Max, in a few weeks I'll be off to college. You keep forgetting. "

"Oh, yes," Max said, suddenly looking at Corliss with a heavy heart. He couldn't believe his best assistant ever was about to leave him. "Are you sure you won't reconsider staying? There's nothing I can do to keep you?"

Corliss shook her head like the good little student she was about to be. "No, Max. I'm closing *The 'Bu* chapter in my life. Two weeks from today I'll be settling into my dorm room at Columbia. It's what I've always dreamed of."

Max felt he was about to say something profound, but he once again got distracted—this time by a trilling coming from his computer. "Corliss, I have to ignore you for a moment.

My dentist just IMed me. He needs to postpone my biweekly teeth whitening appointment, and I have to read him the riot act."

"No worries, Max. I'll just take these magazines outside and burn them."

"Really, Corliss. Don't worry so much about all this. I'm absolutely convinced The 'Bu-hoo will be yesterday's news by the time *The 'Bu* pilot airs. You'll see."

Somewhere in the Woods of Holly—10:29 P.M.

The Bu-Hoo

Hey *'Bu*-sters!

How 'bout ol' Champagne Breath, right? She's like Starlet of the Living Dead. This girl has more lives than a basket full of kittens. She kills!

And she makes MBK's job *sooooooooooo* easy. In fact, there's been another spike in 'Bu-hoo traffic! Twenty-thousand more 'Bu-hoo-bies since her little stunt at the Kodak. Woo-hoo!

Everybody's reading MBK now—thanks to a little free publicity courtesy of Anushka P.! Ha!

I feel so lucky—and you should, too. Ya know why? Because today, *'Bu* babies, I have got triple-decker news. Scream it from the top of the Roosevelt Hotel news. Jump up and down and wet your bikini bottoms news.

I mean, I thought I could keep my piehole shut on this one—to protect those involved. MBK *does* have a heart after all. It might be really, really small—and totally black—but it DOES exist.

So, of course, before I report on anything I factor in the damage it might do to innocent peeps before my typing fingers start tapping! Then I compare the damage factor to the sheer entertainment factor—and guess what? The sheer entertainment factor always wins!

So here we go and drum roll please . . . .

Sources deep inside *'Bu* land tell MBK that none other than that loveable dweeb, JB—aka Jonathan

Bader—is involved in some serious trouble. Don't believe it, you say? Impossible, you protest? Well, *fer shizzle* believe it.

Seems the Jeebster got caught with his hand in the cookie jar. But in this case the cookie jar is his mother's MasterCard! We're not talking a few charges at A/X or H&M. We're talking *thousands of dollars* charged to a certain website.

Nah, it's not one of those dirty sites you can't have access to until you're over eighteen. (Filthy minds!!!) No, the site JB owes money to is something called tradeyourstocks.com. That's where those in the know go to trade in the stock market—but really fast. So fast they can lose their shirts. And pants. And Tweety Bird cotton briefs! Which is exactly what happened to poor Master Bader. He don't know nuttin' about trading stocks! And now he's in deep doo-doo.

But that's not all.

To get his dweeby butt out of hock, he came up with a plan so stupid, so dumb-dumb, so "what the eff were you thinking?" that even MBK is speechless. *He started stealing.* Celebrity stuff. From all the made-for-TV movies he worked on. (You remember those classics: *Brian Hits the Streets, The Mom Committee, Criminal Cul-de-sac.*) He couldn't keep his clammy little hands off his costars' stuff! Stuff like lipstick. Baseball caps. Earrings. Chewed pieces of gum, even! *And then he sold that crap on eBay!*

FOR REALS.

What's that? You don't believe MBK? Well, see below for solid to gold proof! I bid high and caught a rat in the process!

Yours 'Bu-ly,
MBK

"MILEY CYRUS SCRUNCHIE—GOOD AS NEW"

≡ Buy it now!

Meet the Seller

Seller: <u>mileycostar</u> (<u>18</u>) ☆

Here's the rizzle dizzle! Yanked from Miley's ponytail on the set of *Half-Sister Hell*! Will ship worldwide! Priority mail exclusively. Miley doesn't want it back, she swears! Desperate to sell!

J. Bader
P.O. Box 15902
Tarzana, California

Three

Zuma Beach—7:01 A.M., the Next Morning

Corliss thought she might burst. The second episode of *The 'Bu* was about to begin filming. She'd forgotten how excited she'd felt when the pilot episode was shot. A little vibration had begun beneath her ribs, then fluttered its way up into her throat like a hummingbird. And here she was, feeling that little hummingbird feeling all over again.

The actors were in their places in the sand, waiting for Max like good little professionals. They'd moved back into their Canyon condos the night before in order to get up at the buttcrack of dawn so they could be ready for shooting the minute the sun came up.

Tanya wore an ink black Fendi bikini that looked like it was made from about five square inches of fabric. Trent wore teal, pelvis-grazing Marc Jacobs trunks, which made his ice blue eyes pop. And Rocco, bulging from his tree-trunk calves to his foot-wide neck, was packed tightly into a forest green mini-Speedo that set off his midnight-colored hair magnificently.

As Corliss gazed at them, so flawlessly perfect—the sinewy brunette, the blond surfer, the smoldering Mediterranean muscleman—she caught herself sighing a little, then looked around to make sure no one was listening.

"Hey, sighing girl," said JB, who had managed to hear her. "Taking in the view, eh?"

She was about to protest that she was doing no such thing when she felt a tugging on her new Marika Femme capri pants.

"Hey, Corlith."

She looked down. A pint-sized package of terror squinted up at her. "Legend! What are you doing here?"

"Getting a tan before kindergarten." Legend was wearing an L.A. Dodgers baseball cap and a big T-shirt that said SIZE MATTERS.

"JB, you remember Legend."

"Max's stepbrother, right? How are you, little man?"

"Oh, pretty good. But I gueth *you* are not doing tho well."

"Huh?" said JB. "Me? I've never been better. The wind is at my back and the road is . . . er . . . under my car. I can never remember that Irish saying . . ."

Legend frowned. "But what about the controverthy?"

"The what?" said JB, looking at Corliss.

"*Controversy*," Corliss interpreted.

"Thorry, JB. I have a lithp. I have a vocal coach but he thuckth."

"He *sucks*," interpreted Corliss.

"Thanks, Cor, I got that one." JB looked worried.

"But what—what controversy do you speak of, little lisping dude?"

Legend shuffled his feet in the sand and got a sly grin on his face, the one he got whenever he was about to cause trouble.

"Legend," Corliss said in her best former babysitter voice, "are you up to no good? That wouldn't be nice on everyone's first day back to work."

Legend shook his head violently. "No way!"

"Then what are you talking about?"

"Yeah," echoed JB, looking uneasily at Legend.

"Read The 'Bu-hoo!" Legend shouted, then ran toward the catering tent, shaking his pudgy little butt as he went.

JB went white.

"What's the matter, JB?"

"Oh my God, Corliss. Do you think there's anything bad about me on that blog?"

"About *you*? I'm so sure. Like what, you forgot to floss? Come on, JB, Legend can't even read. How could he know what's on that blog?" As soon as Corliss heard herself saying this, she got a sick feeling in her stomach. It was her intuitive side saying something was wrong. She hadn't checked the blog that morning, but someone close to Legend might have. And before she could stop JB, he'd whipped his iPhone out of his board shorts and pulled up TheBuhoo.com.

"JB, *don't*—you know that blog is just trying to cause trouble!"

As JB read, his whiter-than-white face turned pink, then red, then purple. "Oh, God . . ."

"Oh, God, *what*? What does it say?"

"Oh, God, oh, God," JB repeated as he read the blog.

"You're all white . . . like, whiter than usual." It was true. He looked like he was from a long line of extremely white people who kept marrying each other and then giving birth to another generation even whiter than the one before. "JB, what is it?"

"The blog," he said as his teeth began to clatter. "It says—it says—" Before he could finish, his bony knees gave out from under him, and he toppled over, facedown in the sand. Corliss retrieved his iPhone and read what he'd read . . . the scandalous 'Bu-hoo entry about JB's adventures on eBay.

"I'm finished," JB said with a mouthful of sand.

"Hey, Cor!" Tanya yelped as she ran over to where they were. "Hey, JB! What are you doing facedown in the sand?"

Corliss knew she had to cover. "He's, uh, doing some push-ups, Tanya. Come on, JB, just ten more!"

JB tried to lift himself from the ground, but his elbows gave out, and he bit the sand again. Tanya clapped gleefully. "Skinny JB is getting muscles! I so love that!"

"Look, Tanya, why don't you give us a moment here? I'm sort of cardio-training JB, and we're at a critical point with his delt-a-zoids . . ."

"Oh," said Tanya, seeming to buy it. "I totally understand. But when you're done, JB, why don't you come to my trailer? I've got, like, six old scrunchies, all different colors, and you totally won't have to steal them like you did Miley Cyrus's. I could just give them to you! I bet you can get a pretty penny for them on eBay!" Tanya giggled and ran off.

"What in the name of Indiana corn was *that* about?" said Corliss.

"I'm finished," groaned JB. "Cover me in sand and tell everyone I went to Africa and joined the Peace Corps."

"JB, come on, get up. We're about to start shooting."

JB got up on his elbows. "I can't!! I've just been totally exposed on the Internet as a lying, gambling, thieving minor celebrity! *That's* what that was about!"

"Wait—wait—but you're not any of those things, JB! I mean, are you . . . ?"

JB's eyes popped even bigger than they usually popped, and he sputtered and stammered. "Of—of—course they're true! Lying! Thieving! Gambling! Minor celebrity!" He threw himself onto the sand again as if he could eat his way to Africa.

"I see," said Corliss, her mind already racing toward a solution. "Wow. Let me think here . . ."

"Corliss?" It was Max, whispering nearby.

"Yes, Max?"

"Have you seen Legend? He was just in my trailer finger painting with my Aveda flaxseed hair gel, and now I can't find him."

"He ran over to the catering tent, Max. Do you want me to find him?"

"Uh-oh. The catering crew threatened to strike if he ever darkened their tent again. I'll take care of this, Corliss. And I'm sorry he's back on set today. His nanny broke out in some strange rash after he stuffed her bra with gummy bears.

She'll be all right, but she's in an outpatient facility for the next couple days." Max headed toward the catering tent and promptly stumbled over JB. "JB, what are you doing in the sand? We're setting up for the first shot and we can't have you looking *sandy*."

Corliss knew JB was in too delicate a psychological state to defend himself. She'd have to think fast. "Oh, Max, he's just, um, getting prepared for the first scene."

"How does lying facedown in sand prepare him for the first scene?"

"Well, um, yeah. It's very interesting how it does, Max. See, I told JB that since his character Ollie is always, you know, the doormat, he should—as a psychological character exercise—get, like, down on the ground to see what it felt like to be an actual, um, thing people walked on . . . ?" Corliss knew this was totally lame, but she hoped Max would buy it.

"Good thinking, Corliss."

"Thanks. And your hair looks really good today, Max."

"Thank you, I'm completely aware of that. Now please get JB dusted off and in front of the cameras. I'd like to begin." With that, he walked away.

"I'm on it, Max." Corliss helped JB to his feet.

"I'm doomed . . . it's all going dark . . . the end is near . . ."

"Pull yourself together, JB. Just hold your head high. Not everyone believes what they read in that terrible blog."

"Okay," said JB, looking sick. "I'm going to trust you on this one. Even though I know you're just lying to make me feel better."

"I am not," she said, knowing she was lying to make him feel better. "Now come on." She took him by the hand and started walking him over to where Rocco, Tanya, and Trent were ready to start. "Just remember—you are Jonathan Bader, decent guy, talented teen, evolving geek."

JB held his head high. "Okay, Corliss. I'm going to believe what you say. Thanks for bucking me up. I actually feel a whole lot better. See the power you have over evolving geeks everywhere? I'll face my castmates with my evolving geek head held high! They've always respected me. There's no reason to expect they'd treat me any differently now."

"Hey, JB," said Trent as they approached. "Bummer about the, like, gambling, thieving, and minor celeb thing."

"Thanks," said JB weakly, his head no longer held quite so high.

Rocco glared at Trent. "Trent, your behavior is unforgivable. You of all people should know that the dark cloud of scandal touches all of us at some point."

"Whu-ah?" said Trent, scrunching up his eyes in his patented totally-out-of-it look.

"Don't be so gauche, Trent," said Rocco. "JB's soul is in distress. We can't ultimately know what lives in the darkness of men's souls."

"Wha-ha-wa?" said Trent, looking more dumbfounded than ever.

Rocco looked to the sky. "Why has God plunked me down in this land of dunderheads?"

"No need to protect me, Rocs," said JB, like a little soldier. "I deserve all the ribbing I'll no doubt get!"

"Enough," said Max, coming close and dispersing them

with a wave of his hand. "We are all to disregard that hateful blog. *The 'Bu*—our show—the one we've assembled here today to begin filming the second episode of—is bigger than some deranged person's online scribblings. And do you know how I know this?"

The cast stared at him blankly.

"Because my Scientology counselor said so. And immediately after she did she reminded me of my famous phrase."

The cast stared at him blankly again.

"Anyone? My famous phrase . . . ?"

"*The awesomeness of* The 'Bu," supplied Corliss.

"Precisely," said Max, who then looked at everyone again. "So do you know what I did when I was reminded of my famous phrase? . . . Anyone?"

Tanya searched her hair for split ends; Rocco stifled a yawn.

"You, like, wrote it in your iPhone?" asked Trent.

Max narrowed his eyes at Trent. "No. I made a donation of ten thousand dollars for a new Scientology library and thanked my counselor for making me 'clear.' That means I can go to the next Scientology level where people can actually begin to see through me if they look hard enough."

Corliss tugged on Max's sleeve and whispered in his ear. "I think you lost the thread there, Max."

"Right, thanks," he said. "What I mean to say is that the subject of The 'Bu-hoo is *verboten*. Which is German for 'we're not discussing it.' Do we all understand one another?"

Tanya clapped and smiled. "I love German words! I can say *Wiener schnitzel* three times fast!"

"Please don't," said Max, who then looked at Trent. "Do we understand each other?"

"Totally," said Trent. "Sorry, JB."

"No worries, Trent, my dude."

Hey, Max really nipped this in the bud, thought Corliss.

"But if you want, JB," said Trent, "I got a few pairs of old flip-flops in my trailer. They'd for sure pull down a few Gs."

JB looked like he might lose his breakfast.

"All right, enough!" said Max, his voice sliding up into his Mariah Carey upper register. He cleared his throat and continued, now whispering. "Places, people."

"Places, people!" Corliss shouted for those who hadn't heard him.

Max winced. "Corliss, please, sometimes you shout like a deaf umpire on steroids."

"Sorry, Max."

The actors took their places and adjusted what there was of their bathing suits. Hair and makeup people stepped in to do touch-ups on each of them. As they buzzed about the cast, making them prettier and prettier, Max rubbed his hands together and looked at Corliss. She gave him the thumbs-up. His other assistants fanned out behind him and gave him the thumbs-up, too. This bugged Corliss, but at least they weren't making mean faces at her anymore.

"All right. Lovely. Welcome back, everyone. As you know, there are very high hopes for our pilot episode, which airs in two weeks. The UBC network is pouring millions of dollars into publicity, which includes cheap T-shirts people will be able to buy on Melrose. Your faces are, as we speak, being plastered across billboards high over Sunset Boulevard and buses in New York City. There are even talks of anatomically correct action figures. In other words, before it's even on the air, *The 'Bu* will be big."

"I've, like, been hearing industry buzz all summer," Trent said, cleaning his ear with his finger.

"Trent," said Max, "zip it with the surfer mouth." Trent zipped it. "But, yes, what Trent says is true. We are, apparently, the talk of TV Land."

The cast looked jazzed. Corliss felt that hummingbird of excitement fly up into her head and do circles.

"Of course, what all of this means is that we will have to *deliver*. Our second episode must top our first. Which is why we hired back our excellent head writer, Petey Newsome." Max gestured to Petey who was standing nearby.

The cast applauded. Petey, dressed in his usual mortician-like uniform, squinted and shook his head modestly. Then he winked at Corliss. Corliss smiled back painfully.

"And to make sure the scripts continue to *deliver*, Petey and I recently hand-selected a bunch of A-list writers for our new staff." Max pointed to a scraggly-looking group of peckish-looking, poorly dressed people with anxious looks on their faces. They slouched and scowled and squeaked out some *Hi's* in unison.

Max winced. Probably because physically unattractive people made him uncomfortable. "They may not be runway-ready, cast, but their *minds* are beautiful." He winced at the writers again.

"Thanks for the vote of confidence, Max," droned Petey, who then looked over at Corliss and smiled. Corliss pretended she was looking somewhere else. *Blech—why is he always smiling at me like some creepy old man when, in fact, he's a creepy young man, about my same age?*

Max clapped his hands a few times. "Very good. Now let us begin. The first scene up is between Rocco and Tanya's characters—Ramone and Tessa. As you know from reading the script, it's a hot, steamy love scene."

Tanya jumped up and down. "Hot, steamy love!"

Trent's face went pink as Tanya licked her sun-kissed lips and looked sexily in Rocco's direction. Rocco looked back and stifled a yawn.

"Calm down, Tanya," said Max. "Save your excitement for *the scene*."

"Yes, Max," said Tanya, tucking her hands under her armpits. "And I remember that the word *act* is in the word *action*—which is so helpful for me because then when you say the word 'action,' I remember the little word inside the big word, and I do it."

"Brilliant," said Max, not hiding his sarcasm. He turned to Rocco. "And when I say *action*, Rocco, I want your character, Ramone, to be on Tanya's character, Tessa, like—like—" Max seemed lost. "Corliss, I need a metaphor . . . how should Ramone be on Tessa?"

"Like bananas on an ice-cream sundae?"

"Sure, why not? Rocco and Tanya, do you two understand the imagery?"

Rocco sighed. "I understand literary devices, Max, no matter how hackneyed or trite they may be."

"I do, too!" yelped Tanya. "I understand literary devices! Ramone is, like, a banana, and Tessa is like the ice-cream sundae underneath. All, like, gooey and yummy with a big banana on top of her. Right?"

Max mopped sweat off his brow. "Yes, something like that, Tanya. Just find your mark, and we'll take it from there."

Rocco stifled another yawn. Tanya clapped some more and then moved close to Rocco so she could stand on her mark. Corliss couldn't help but notice Trent's face was all scrunched up, and his eyes were tiny. He was glaring at Tanya and staring daggers through Rocco. *If he were a cartoon character, he'd have steam coming out of his ears!* Maybe because The 'Bu-hoo had mentioned over the summer that Tanya and Rocco had been seen at Beyonce's birthday party looking extremely close?

"Places, people!" Max began pacing back and forth in the sand. His assistants followed him, fanning out in a perfect V formation, except for Corliss, who thought they were all nuts.

The actors took their places. Corliss felt that little hummingbird again—which promptly flew away when Petey sidled up to her. "Hey, Corliss."

"Oh, hi, Petey," she said, whispering, hoping to bring his volume down by example. She knew Max was getting into his "directing zone," *and* she felt a little oogy around Petey. There was just something about him that ratcheted up her oog factor. He'd also sent her e-mails all summer, but she'd never returned one. Not one! She didn't want to encourage his crush, which didn't seem based on anything except for the fact that she was the only one who ever stood up for him.

"I've missed you," Petey said, a little too loudly.

"Shh!" Corliss pointed at Max in his zone.

"I've missed you," Petey now whispered.

"Really?" Corliss whispered back with a fake smile. (Uncle Ross had taught her how to fake smile that very weekend.)

"Really?" Petey said, grinning a hopeful grin.

"Oh, that's, um, really unnecessary, Petey."

Petey looked hurt. "It is?"

"I mean, that's really *sweet*. I meant to say *sweet*—before I said *unnecessary* which came out of, like, a dark place in my head I have no control over." She realized Petey was making her feel totally uncomfortable—which was why she couldn't stop talking. "In psychology terms that place is called the *id*, which is, like, the childlike part of the brain that just says *blah, blah, blah* whatever it wants and . . ."

She was blathering on, but Petey didn't seem to care. "I could listen to you shoot off your mouth like an auctioneer all day," said Petey.

"Shh, Petey, seriously. Max is about to begin." Just as she said it, Max stepped up and lifted one manicured hand in the air.

"Places please, everyone," said Max. "Cameras are rolling!"

Everyone got quiet. Petey waved bye-bye to Corliss and finally moved away. A production assistant stepped in with the clapper. "*The 'Bu* . . . episode two . . . take one!" She clapped the clapper and Corliss's heart leaped. It was finally happening. After months and months, the second episode was about to begin filming. And even though all Corliss thought about these days was heading off to college, she couldn't imagine any place she'd rather be than right here, right now. As the cameras started to roll, and the gorgeous actors began to speak, Corliss chanted Max's catchphrase in her head: *the awesomeness of* The 'Bu!

"And we're . . . rolling!" said Max.

★ The 'Bu

EXT. MALIBU BEACH—DAWN

SEAGULLS soar placidly over the morning
surf. The SUN rises over Malibu Canyon. We
TILT DOWN to find TWO BODIES intertwined in
the sand.

CAMERA PUSHES IN on TESSA and RAMONE. Sand
dapples their bronzed limbs as they stare
into each other's eyes.

                TESSA
    Oh God . . .

                RAMONE
    What is it?

Tessa searches for the words—any words—to
describe how she feels.

                TESSA
    It's just . . . the world! It's
    changed so much in such a short
    period of time. Am I the only one
    who feels that?

                    RAMONE
          Of course not.

                    TESSA
          It's amazing . . . but terrible,
          too.

Ramone looks away. He can't seem to bear
this kind of talk.

                    RAMONE
          I only want to be happy, Tessa.

                    TESSA
          I know. But I mean . . . just a
          few weeks ago I was with Travis.

                    RAMONE
          And I was with . . . Alecia.

Ramone closes his eyes to keep tears from
forming.

                    TESSA
          Now Travis has been reassigned to
          another beach . . .

                    RAMONE
         . . . and Alecia's been
         reassigned *to heaven.*

They cling to each other and begin kissing.
Slowly at first, but then their passion
becomes ferocious. Finally, Tessa pulls
away.

                    TESSA
         Something about this has to be
         wrong!

Ramone takes her by the shoulders.

                    RAMONE
         Look into my eyes, Tessa.

She does; she can't look away.

                    RAMONE (cont.)
         Is what you see there "wrong"?
         Is what you feel when we hold
         each other "wrong"? Would Alecia
         begrudge me the chance to love

again?

                    TESSA
        I guess not . . . she loved you
        too much.

                    RAMONE
        And would Travis begrudge *you*?

Tessa detaches herself from him, sits up,
looks far out to the horizon.

                    TESSA
            That's just it, Ramone. I think
            Travis might still be in love
            with me.

Ramone's face falls.

                    RAMONE
            And you? Are you still in love
            with *him*? Tell me, Tessa. I need
            to know.

                    TESSA
            (after a long moment)
            I can't tell you, Ramone. I don't
            know myself . . .

FADE OUT.

Somewhere in the Valley—3:45 P.M.

The Bu-Hoo

'*Bu* bay-hay-bees!

I don't know what to say. It's like God is smiling down on MBK these days. Everywhere I turn there's dirt on the babes in '*Bu*-land.

But first you gots to know the UBC network is promoting *The 'Bu* like it's the next-generation iPhone. It's getting a fabulous time slot, big splashy promotions, and miles and miles of ink. No expenses are being spared to catapult this teen beach sex weeper to the top of the ratings heap! HOLLA!

But that's not why I write today. Oh no. What I've got for you is much BIGGER news. News that will impact *The 'Bu* immediately—and profoundly.

FILE UNDER: California crazy talk.

I had to consult with a few HIGHLY PLACED sources on this one—but what I'm about to tell you *fer shizzle* checks out. Trent Owen Michaels, one-time star of the short-lived CW show *Emo Surfer*, and virginity-buster of starlets up and down the California coast, has got a secret.

No, the dude ain't gay. Or really a woman. Or a rocket scientist masquerading as a dumb-dumb. No, no. SOOO much more delish! Seems Mr. Michaels has been fighting to keep something down for a looooong time. Or maybe he *hasn't* been able to keep it down . . . ? Heck, I can't keep it down any longer so I might as well let it out!

The dude's on Jenny Craig.

JENNY EFFIN' CRAIG!!!!!

Has been since he was twelve. That's when he blew up like a blond bowling ball and his mother

(Miss San Dimas of 1983) said, "No way! I refuse to have a little tubby-wubby for a son!" So she called up Jenny. If he so much as goes off that diet, he's sunk like a three hundred pound wet suit.

That's why y'all should know surfer boy had a few slips over the summer when *The 'Bu* actors were on hiatus. Gained about two inches around the middle. But now that the cameras are rolling again he's more committed than ever to keeping that six-pack ripped.

BUT. He's got his *triggers*—which means things that make him dream of ice cream, Yodels, and those puffy pink things with coconut sprinkled all over them. And one of those triggers is the thought of his former GF Tanya Ventura getting it on with another guy. In this case, one Rocco DiTullio. If Trent thinks this love affair is real, he might start reaching for the Ho Hos!

But is it real?? The rizzle dizzle?? No one's saying. Sure, Tanya and Rocco's tongues did the saliva dance onscreen while filming the second episode, but have they done it *off*? If not, will they? More important, will Trent be able to keep out of Taco Bell's drive-through window?

Stay tuned 'Bu-sters!

Yours 'Bu-lemicly,
MBK

Four

Trent's Condo, Malibu Canyon—the Next Morning

Corliss knocked again. But still no answer. "Trent? Trent! Come on, you've got to be in there. Your call is in fifteen, and I'm here to pick you up. Trent?"

Nothing. Corliss looked at her watch. Maybe he'd gone surfing and lost track of the time? Trent had done this before. The last time it happened, ten production assistants were sent out in wetsuits to scour the coastline. But when two ended up needing CPR, the network decided the insurance for "Trent searches" was way too high. Thereafter, they paid for a waterproof cell phone that attached to Trent's surfboard.

Corliss took out her phone and found TRENT'S SURFBOARD. She made the call, but it went straight to voicemail. "Hi, Trent, this is Corliss leaving a message. I'm here at your condo to pick you up for your call, but where are *you*? Can you please ring me when you get this? Thanks."

This was one of those terribly *un*-glamorous 'Bu moments that made Corliss glad she was heading off to college. *Getting actors to the set on time is like trying to herd gerbils!* she thought.

Her phone rang back. But it wasn't Trent. It was Max. She answered it promptly. "Hi, what's up?"

"Corliss, it's Max."

"I know."

"You do?"

"Yes, I saw your name on caller ID."

"You did?"

"Yes, Max, we've been through this. Your phone does it, too. But you have to *look* at it when it rings."

"Corliss, you know I have an assistant who handles my phone. *He's* the one who looks at it, and I'm not sure I even know what *he* looks like, let alone the phone. But enough about technological advancements; we need Trent on set pronto."

"But Max—"

"I want a more lifelike hermit crab scar on Trent, and the makeup people say they aren't miracle workers; they need more time, a larger trailer, an air purifier, blah blah blah. Can you believe the demands of unionized people?"

"But Max, I can't—"

"Please, Corliss, the hermit crab scar Trent now has isn't fooling anyone. It looks like a hickey."

"It probably is," Corliss said under her breath.

"I heard that, Corliss. I don't appreciate your withering comments so early in the day."

"Sorry."

"Look, all the production assistants are tied up trying to get me a Pinkberry with pineapple, and I'm a little on the verge of cranky. You're supposed to be picking Trent up, anyway. Is there a problem?

Corliss knew better than to worry Max. "Uh, no. No problem, Max. It's just—"

"No 'just,' Corliss. I simply need you to get Trent to the set ASAP. Now I'm going to hand my phone to my phone assistant who will do something to it so it goes away."

The line went dead.

Malibu Seafood—11:23 A.M.

Corliss had spent the last forty-five minutes asking surfers up and down the coast if they'd seen Trent. None had. But she did manage to get two phone numbers and a compliment on her Juicy Couture sundress.

It didn't matter, though. The whole process made her feel humiliated. Hadn't she proven to Max that she was above tracking down lost actors? Wasn't she now on salary to do legitimate work for *The 'Bu*? And what was all that about "Is there anything I can do to change your mind about college, Corliss? You're indispensable to me." If all he was going to do was use her to track down lost actors, she might as well get on the plane today. *Show business can be so degrading!*

More than degraded, Corliss was *starving*. Lucky for her, she spotted Malibu Seafood up ahead. She figured some fried catfish slathered in tartar sauce should hit the spot. But as she pulled into the parking lot and headed to the take-out window, she heard her Uncle Ross's voice in her head. "Corliss, on the coasts we prefer to have our fish raw. Sushi, sashimi, ceviche. Fried fish is only for those poor souls who live *in the middle of the country.*" Good thing Uncle Ross was miles away.

"Fried catfish and fries!" she ordered. As she waited, her phone trilled in her purse. She saw it was Anushka. She debated on whether or not to pick it up—they hadn't talked since the Kodak Theater debacle, and Corliss was still pretty miffed. *Better just get it out in the open,* Corliss thought as she answered.

"Hey, Anushka."

"Cor! Where you been, girl?"

"To tell you the truth, Anushka—"

"Listen, I'm a little bit desperate here . . ."

Corliss could hear the panic in Anushka's voice. "You didn't shave your head, did you?"

"NO, God . . . I might be nuts, but I'm not crazy! It's *school.* You know that hot professor I told you about? The one with the big nose?"

"Anushka, I'm kinda on the clock here and—"

"Okay, don't matter. Wait, where are you?"

"Malibu Seafood, but—"

"Yum! Love that place. Anyway, listen, so Big Nose assigned this reading assignment over the summer, something about brain ventricles—*whatever*—and we're supposed to discuss it the first day of class, which is all of a sudden *tomorrow*!"

"Anushka, tomorrow can't be all of a sudden. It pretty much always follows *today.*"

"But I'm totally barfing, Cor! I read the thing last night, and I don't get it!"

"Not any of it?"

"No! Zero, zilch, squat of it!"

"Anushka, I'd be glad to help but—"

"Really? You're the bestest best!! I'm on Montana; I can be there in ten." The line went dead.

Why is my life filled with people who make strange requests and then hang up on me before I get a chance to tell them to take a hike?

But Corliss's self-flagellation was short-lived because her catfish and fries had arrived. They were nestled in a little paper bowl. Steam wafted up into her nostrils, and she swooned from the smell of warm, fishy goodness. As she headed to the picnic area she thought, *This I do for myself.* After all, she couldn't search for Trent on an empty stomach, could she? She took a seat at a picnic table and looked out at the hundreds of surfers speckling the Pacific Ocean. She shook her head. *Does Max think I have superpowers? Trent could be any of those dopes!*

But as she savored the deep-fried batter of her catfish, and the mushy, salty fries, which were now smothered in ketchup and hot sauce, something caught her eye in the dunes next to the picnic area. Something sticking up out of the sand. *A surfboard.* With a painting of Eve in the Garden of Eden on it. A snake covered her naughty bits, and then curled up over her head and wrapped around the tip of the board. This could have been *any* surfer dude's board except for the fact that Eve looked suspiciously like . . . *Tanya Ventura.*

Corliss squinted. *Fried cheese on a sand dune, that IS Tanya Ventura!*

She shoved the rest of her catfish into her mouth (and dipped a few more fries into ketchup and hot sauce and downed those, too) and headed into the dunes toward the board.

What she saw there took her breath away. Hidden behind the surfboard, looking up at her with big eyes—and flecks of fried fish mashed all over the lower end of his tanned face—was Trent Owen Michaels.

"Trent, my God!"

Tears formed in his sky blue eyes. "Corliss, what are you doing here?"

"Trent, forget about me. What are *you* doing here? You're supposed to be on set!"

"It's not, like, what it looks like . . ."

"I'm not sure what it looks like, except *gross*. What's going on? Did you have a drastic dip in blood sugar?"

Trent lowered his eyes. "I guess you haven't read The 'Bu-hoo."

"No, I hate that blog! Why?"

"Because now it says . . ." he looked up through his sun-bleached bangs, ". . . like, bad things about me."

Corliss threw her hands in the air. "What now? And why do you people keep reading that thing? It's totally eats away at everyone's self-esteem—which is extremely dangerous for people in the entertainment industry!"

Trent tilted his head like a five-year-old who's just been asked to do calculus.

"Sorry," said Corliss, who realized she had forgotten her audience. "It's *bad* for you!"

"Whatevs. Everyone knows now." Trent sniffled and used his fingers to eat some of the coleslaw that had fallen onto his board shorts. "And everyone's gonna tell everyone they know. But they don't know *why* they know what they know."

"Use your words, Trent! I'm totally lost."

"I have," he stifled back a sob, "an eating disorder."

Corliss was mystified. *He has a what? He can't! His body is flawless.* "You? But you're like the fat-free-est guy I know. You're like tone-o-rama!"

"Maybe," he said, flexing one pec, then another, then both really rapidly (his signature move in the opening credits of *Emo Surfer*). "But that's only because I've been on Jenny Craig since I was fifteen."

Now Corliss was *really* confused.

"Yup, Trent Owen Michaels took the Jenny challenge."

Corliss turned away. She had to so she wouldn't laugh. *Isn't Jenny Craig for old, fat housewives who spend all day salivating over Rachael Ray's recipes?* She composed herself and turned back to Trent. "I'm so sorry to hear that, Trent. The eating disorder thing—not the Jenny Craig thing."

"Yeah, but now I'm totally *off* Jenny Craig. Which happens during, um, what they call—wait, let me think—" Corliss could tell he was struggling. "I got it! It happens during *times of stress*. Like when I'm all, like, *whoa, what's happening?* about something. Which in this case is, like, being totally outed as a stud who's on an old lady's diet program."

"Wow, that's terrible." Corliss felt truly bad. First, JB's exposure as a day-trading teen and eBay crook, and now this. Was the entire cast falling to pieces? "Anything I can help you with? I mean, I *am* about to begin my undergraduate degree in the psychology department of Columbia University," she said with pride. "I do understand people's natures and, to a certain extent, the powerful pull of addiction."

Trent shook his head. He looked desolate. "Nope,

nothing. It's up to me. I just have to realize a power greater than me. And it's usually something fried."

"Trent," she said with the practiced tenderness of a budding psychiatrist. "I appreciate your efforts at self-improvement and applaud your fortitude."

"Corliss, you *totally* have to bring down the SAT words."

"Sorry. What I mean is—"

But she was cut off by a familiar husky voice, which came from behind them. "What she means is she thinks you're on the right track, sandbar boy." It was Anushka. She was wearing BCBG hot pants with cork-heeled sandals, a lacy Stella McCartney spaghetti-strap T, and blackout Ray-Ban aviators. "What are you kids doing out here in the dunes?"

"Hey, Anushka," said Trent, who looked less than thrilled to see her.

"That's the hello I get?"

"Anushka!" Corliss hugged her, forgetting in a flash how miffed she was the instant she saw her gorgeous friend.

"That's more like it," said Anushka hugging her back. "Look, I bet everyone hates me for what I said on *Access Hollywood*. You know, about everyone on *The 'Bu* being all nuts or something. But it was *such* a crazy scene that night with all the paparazzi all over me, just *dying* to hear what I had to say, and I was *totally* caught off guard."

Corliss knew Anushka was full of it. Anushka knew *exactly* what she was doing that night at the Kodak—getting herself the press she couldn't live without. And also getting back at Max, which seemed to be her unspoken goal since she got fired from the show. But Corliss also knew she couldn't keep a grudge where Anushka was concerned. They'd been through too much. And the truth was, Anushka, for all her faults, had always been loyal to her—in her own unique way. "Let's talk about that later, Anushka. Right now I've got to get some Wetnaps, clean Trent up, and get him to the set ASAP."

"I've got Wetnaps in my limo," Anushka offered.

"You do?"

"Well, baby wipes actually. Same dif. Come on, you two. Why don't I hook you both up with a ride back to the set? Trent can wipe himself down, and the chauffeur can haul some serious 'Bu butt—certainly faster than your little Mazda, Cor, and whatever surfer piece of crapola 4 x 4 Trent is currently driving. My chauffeur *never* drives the speed limit."

"That's great, Anushka—thanks!"

Trent pouted and sucked the remaining tartar sauce off his fingernails. "I don't wanna."

Anushka rolled her eyes. "Come on, Trent, let me help you out. You don't want to incur the wrath of Max Marx, do you? Look what happened to me. He canned my million dollar heinie!"

Trent shook his head back and forth like a little boy.

Corliss was now officially at her wits' end. "Trent, seriously—we should go with Anushka. Max is going to hit the roof as it is! I can cover for you, but let's move, okay?"

Corliss tugged at him, but he kept sitting in the sand and shaking his head. Then he curled his lip at Anushka, which she responded to by flipping him the bird.

"God! What is it between you two, anyway?" asked Corliss. "You're always making faces at each other, like, 'Ick, I hate that person's face.'"

"Care to enlighten little Miss Meyers?" said Anushka, putting a hand on her hip and cocking an eyebrow.

"Nuh-uh," said Trent, pouting in the sand.

"Fine!" said Anushka, flipping him two birds now.

"Jeez," said Corliss. "All this rage! You two act like you were married or something."

Anushka put a finger down her throat as a response. "Please, Cor, don't make me gag."

"Yeah, me too," said Trent.

"It did *not* get that far, Cor. Let's just say when I was on *Suburban Magic* and Trent was on *Emo Surfer*, our agents had the bright idea to—I'm gagging again—set us up. To generate a little extra publicity or *something*. So, fine, whatever. I said, 'Sure, I'll have *one date* with some mouth-breathing merman.'"

"Hey!" said Trent, who seemed genuinely hurt.

"I mean, who doesn't want to date a guy who grunts and scored 420 combined on his SATs?"

"You seemed to want to date me that night!"

Corliss couldn't believe it. These two had actually *dated*??

"Puh-lease. I did NOT want to date you that night. You took me to *Jamba Juice*. Ha! Like buying me a Protein Berry Workout Smoothie is a date."

"But I paid for a fiber boost!"

Anushka rolled her eyes. "Just what every girl wants on a date—a happy colon."

"Some girls do!" Trent yelled.

"Guys, guys!" Corliss said, stepping between them before it got really ugly. "We have to get Trent to the set! Trent, your surfboard will fit in Anushka's limo, *and* she has baby wipes. You're covered in condiments, and you should have been on set an hour ago! What part of 'get your sun-drenched head to the set' don't you understand?!"

"Fine," huffed Trent.

"Fine," huffed Anushka. "But wait a second . . ."

"*You now?*" pleaded Corliss. "Come on, we really have to go!"

"Okay, jeez. Just one question, Cor."

"What is it?" said Corliss, tugging Anushka and Trent toward Anushka's limo.

"Are those Tanya's naked boobies on that surfboard?"

The '*Bu* Set/Malibu Beach—11:47 A.M.

Max felt a shiver run up the back of his knees. An immaculately detailed stretch limo was pulling into the parking lot off Pacific Coast Highway. *Please, no, don't let it be . . .* This was exactly Michael Rothstein's method of sneak attack.

"Where is that thing I asked for that I really need?" he whispered to his assistants, pointing this way and that, sending them scurrying all over for something they were too scared to ask him to identify. Max was trying to look in control so that, as Michael approached, he would sense a beehive of activity. But when Max looked back at the parking lot, he saw *Corliss* stepping out of the limo.

What is Corliss doing with Michael Rothstein? When Trent followed Corliss out of the limo, Max's heart thumped like a Congo drum. *Dear God, has Corliss sold me out to Michael Rothstein?!* When Anushka emerged from the limo,

Max almost fainted. *Sweet Scientology, NO! Anushka has engineered this whole thing to reveal me as incompetent to Michael Rothstein so she can get back on the show!*

He held his breath as he waited for Michael Rothstein to step out. But Michael Rothstein did not step out. Instead, Anushka kissed Corliss on the cheek and retreated into the limo, closing the door behind her. Off the limo went, slithering down PCH toward Venice Beach.

Max heaved a huge sigh.

"Hey, Max!" shouted Corliss as she approached. "I found him!"

Trent trailed a few feet behind Corliss, his head hung low. "Sorry, Max. See, what happened was—"

"Trent," said Max, "one moment please. I need to speak rather forcefully to Corliss right now."

"What is it, Max? I found Trent, didn't I? I know we're late but—"

"Corliss, yes, you did find Trent. He smells a little like baby wipes but at least he's here."

Trent shrugged. "I had to wipe myself."

Max didn't want to know any more. "Trent, please head directly to hair and makeup. They want to redo that hermit crab scar you have on your thigh. They say it looks like a hickey."

"But that mark on my thigh *is* a hickey."

Max held up his talk-to-the-hand. "Trent, to hair and makeup, please."

Trent slunk off.

"Where did you find him, Corliss?"

"At Malibu Seafood."

Max feared the worst. "He wasn't . . . gorging himself, was he?"

Corliss nodded. "It was pretty sad, Max. I think Trent has a real problem."

"Then the latest entry on The 'Bu-hoo is true."

"Hey, that kinda rhymes!"

"Corliss, I don't appreciate your levity at a time that should be un . . . leavened."

"Sorry, Max, just trying to interject some humor here. Look, the good news is I think Trent *knows* he's got a problem. He's just really embarrassed that everyone else knows—thanks to that stupid blog."

"Hmmm. I wonder if I should refer Trent to my Scientology counselor."

"Max, I'm sorry, but the last thing Trent needs is help from a cult of Hollywood zombies. What he *really* needs is understanding."

"Good point, Corliss. Even though you've deftly buried a critique of my religion somewhere in there."

Corliss smiled sheepishly.

"But here's the thing, Corliss—Trent Owen Michaels is a heartthrob. That's why we hired him. That's why girls scream when he appears on the red carpet. That's why some shirtless—and pantless—photos of him are all over the Web. And, as everyone knows, heartthrobs *can't be fat*. Once they're fat they have to do comic turns in B movies. They have to make strange faces and gestures."

"Um, I think I see your point, Max. But what can we do about it? It's not like we can chain ourselves to Trent to watch what he eats."

"Of course we can't, but we *can* make Trent extremely self-conscious about his diet whenever he's around us. Really monitor every little thing he eats. Nit and pick and criticize."

Corliss scrunched up her face. "Max, I don't think that's the way to deal with—"

"Don't worry, Corliss, I'll put two of my most hyper-critical assistants on it. He'll be shamed into staying thin—which is how most people do it. *You* I need for something far more important. In fact, a crucial final mission before—before—"

"Before I go off to college?"

Max nodded sadly.

"Phew! A crucial assignment! I was beginning to think I'd spend my last week on *The 'Bu* chasing down surfers. Not that I mind—I did get two numbers and a compliment on my Juicy top—"

"Corliss, please, TMI. I can't be expected to engage with you about your thriving, post-geek social life."

"Gotcha."

"And, just so you know, every time you say the phrase 'going off to college,' it's as if a pit bull lunges for my neck, tears at my carotid artery, and sucks the life from me."

"Vivid imagery, Max, but I think what you're expressing is that you'll miss me."

Max pretended he hadn't heard her. "I'm sorry, Corliss, what? I was looking at my cuticles. They are exceptional this week."

"Of course they are," said Corliss, sighing. "So what is

this 'crucial' final mission, Max?"

"Right—thank you. What you must do is *find out who is writing this blog*. Bad publicity is one thing, but when it starts affecting the morale of my cast, that's where I put my foot down. Did you notice my new Bruno Maglis by the way?" he said, beveling his foot to show her.

"But Max—"

"Corliss, I'd say 'please cease' but I don't say that anymore. This is of the utmost importance. Someone involved at the highest levels of *The 'Bu* is writing this blog or feeding information to the person who is writing it. That person has to be ferreted out like a—like a—"

"Ferret?"

"Exactly. Like the beady-eyed little creature that he or she is. This 'Bu-hoo business has gone way too far. I want you on the case. If you have any reservations, please express them now."

"Look, Max, I agree the blog is a terrible thing. I even see how it's affecting the psychological well-being of our cast. But what you're asking me to do is exactly the same thing I was doing for you when I first started working with you, and I had to be all lurky-loo around Trent and Tanya. All that spying makes me go crazy!"

"But Corliss—"

"I'll have to be up in my friends' business—"

"But Corliss—"

"I'll have to be skulking around in potted plants—"

"But Corliss!"

"I'll have to be pretending to be in love with TV stars with eating disorders!"

"Corliss, please! I realize what I'm asking you."

"I don't think you do, Max. I don't want to head off to school known as 'Corliss Meyers, Secret Agent.'"

"Hear me out. Whoever is writing The 'Bu-hoo is exposing the secrets of semifamous people for their own thrills. That is a criminal act with upsetting psychological ramifications, don't you agree?"

"Well . . ."

"Which means that the person is criminally insane, right?"

"I guess . . ."

"And isn't your life's goal, Corliss Meyers, to *help* insane people?"

"Yes, but—"

"Then if you uncover the person behind that blog, we can put an end to this madness, help your friends who are undergoing extreme psychological stress, *and* help someone who is deeply troubled get the psychological counseling they need."

Max could tell Corliss was mulling this over. He took this moment to pick two grains of sand from his Yves Saint Laurent polo.

"You know what, Max? You're right. Whoever is writing this blog is obviously extremely disturbed."

"Exactly!"

"Someone with anger issues who's acting out."

"Now you're seeing it, Corliss."

"Someone who needs *my help*."

"I couldn't have put it better myself. You are in a unique position to assist many people in psychological distress—me at the top of the list. Now do you see how crucial a mission this is?"

Corliss nodded gravely. "Okay, Max. You're on. I'll find out who MBK is or my name isn't Corliss Beverly Meyers!"

"Beverly?"

"Yes, but forget I said that. And I want to do this my way. I don't want to compromise my ideals, or put myself in any awkward positions. Remember, even though I've kinda pulled it together, style-wise, at heart I'm still just a goody-goody honors student from Indiana-no-place."

"Believe me," Max said, looking her up and down, "that's clear to all of us, Corliss. And I promise—*no awkward positions*. It's a deal."

Pizzeria Mozza—7:21 P.M.

"Corliss," said Uncle Ross, "you're not eating the squash blossoms." Before them were six gorgeous yellow squash blossoms, stuffed with ricotta cheese and fried in parmesan bread crumbs. Uncle Ross popped one in his mouth and moaned in pleasure. Corliss looked out the window. "What is it? I hope nothing's wrong with my favorite niece?"

"Uncle Ross, I'm your *only* niece."

"You are? But who's that other girl in your house whenever I visit?"

"Hello! That's my *mother*."

"Oh, right. You'll have to forgive me, Corliss; women are sort of a vague blur for me. Like in movies where people take the wrong medicine and suddenly everything goes swirly?" He winked at one of the busboys and Corliss rolled her eyes.

"I'll make a note of that, Uncle Ross."

"Besides, what does any of this have to do with you refusing to eat the squash blossoms?"

"I'm just preoccupied, Uncle Ross. First, I'm not entirely sure why anyone would eat a squash blossom, let alone one filled with ricotta cheese."

"But these are delectable!" Uncle Ross made a tsk-tsk sound and ate another squash blossom.

"I'm also trying to figure out who is writing this blog."

"Which blog? The one about that delicious Eric Mabius on *Ugly Betty*?"

"No, Uncle Ross, The 'Bu-hoo. The blog about the show *I'm* working on? The blog that's been making my life miserable and destroying the lives of several of the actors on *The 'Bu*?"

"Corliss, your tendency to overemphasize is exhausting."

"Sorry. It's just I'm all worked up. Do you have any advice?"

"Maybe Eric Mabius could do a guest spot on your show?"

"How does that help anything?"

"I'm not sure, but I have a feeling he'd look *tres* fetching on a beach."

Corliss sighed. "I'll make a note of *that*, too, Uncle Ross. I'll put it next to your Zac Efron guest star suggestion."

"There's no reason to be snippy, Corliss. I just have

an eye for talent. And besides, I thought you kept telling everyone not to pay attention to that blog. What gives?"

"I *was* telling everyone that! But ever since Anushka blabbed about The 'Bu-hoo on national television, it's like that blog is required reading for the entire country! It's gotten gazillions of hits a day since then, and the pilot hasn't even aired. *And* the cast is totally strung out because all their personal secrets are now being revealed."

"I'm so sorry to hear that," said Uncle Ross as a server dropped another tray of appetizers on their table. "Ooh, the chicken liver bruschetta, Corliss! It is *to die for.*"

But Corliss didn't care about another plate of appetizers; she hadn't even touched the first. She was too busy thinking about who could be writing the blog. "Well, the fact of the matter is, I told Max that I'd help him find out who this MBK person is. In fact, it's my last assignment for him before I go off to college. And probably my most important since I started working on *The 'Bu.*"

"Okay, Corliss, I see you're going to be utterly distracted until you crack this blog thing. Let Uncle Ross help. Who is at the top of your list of suspects? And it better not be me."

Corliss had a terrible feeling. *It might be Uncle Ross! He can't keep a secret, and he has an adolescent curiosity for all things unsavory and salacious.* She decided to grill him a little to see if her suspicions had any merit. But she knew she'd have to be clever about it so he wouldn't catch on. "Oh, let's talk about something else, Uncle Ross. We're at an amazing restaurant and here I am talking about business!"

"A change of topic is always fine by me, Corliss," said Uncle Ross, cramming another piece of bruschetta in his mouth. "What would you like to talk about?"

"Well, I don't know . . . stuff I've always wondered about you. Like how much time do you spend on the computer?"

"What? On the computer? Oh, I don't know. I do a lot of shopping on the computer and, well, going from website to website—Web cruising, as they say. But only to kill time when Jurgen's at the salon."

"And would you say you have a big or little interest in the lives of teenage television stars?"

"These are strange questions, Corliss. But I'd say I have a healthy interest in teenage TV stars for a man my age. Not too big, but not too little, either. I do like to keep up with kid culture."

Corliss was growing worried by his incriminating responses. She knew she had to go in for the kill. "And just how much of a snoop would you say you are when it comes to other people's personal lives?"

"Corliss, so many questions! It's like the Spanish Inquisition here. Wait a minute! You don't think *I'm* writing that odious little blog, do you?"

"I'm sorry, Uncle Ross, but I do tell you everything. Which means you have a lot of information about what goes on at *The 'Bu*. It *could* be you."

"Corliss, you know I only pay attention to about half of anything you're ever talking about. Also, I retain nothing."

"Yup, both things true," Corliss had to admit.

"And, of course, *you're* the one who knows everything about *The 'Bu*. Any reasonable person might conclude that *you* are the author of that notorious blog."

Corliss couldn't believe her uncle would think such a thing. Before she could protest, the waitress arrived in a crisp white smock. Her sun-streaked hair poked into her eyes, and she had the glazed look of someone who'd just been yelled at. "Have you decided on your entrees?"

"Yes," said Uncle Ross. "I'll have the fennel sausage, panna, and spring onion pizza. My niece will have the wild spinach, nettles, nostrano, and cacio di Roma pizza."

"I will? The only thing I recognized in there was the word *spinach*."

Uncle Ross ignored her. "Also, another glass of this delicious Rosso Piceno. In fact, whenever you see the glass empty, please feel free to fill it. I'd order a glass for my niece here but she simply *refuses* to drink underage."

"Very good," said the waitress, who seemed to be fighting back tears as she disappeared into the dinner throng.

"Uncle Ross, I can assure you, it's not me who's writing the blog, even though Max thought so at one point. Can you believe? I mean I've been a double agent but I'm fairly certain I don't have the energy to be a triple agent."

"You never know until you try, dear girl. It's certainly not me, however. I couldn't be less interested in the comings and goings of a bunch of post-pubescent horn toads with gorgeous faces and bodies and too much cash and time on their hands." Uncle Ross then got a strange look on his face. "Wait, I *am* interested in those things . . ."

"Don't worry, I know it's not you, Uncle Ross. It's got to be someone in the cast—or real close. I keep thinking

it's JB. Even though he's my closest friend on the show."
As Uncle Ross polished off what was left of the bruschetta,
Corliss thought about what on earth could be JB's motivation
to write such a blog. "JB is always online because of his
day trading problem, which has forced him into debt and
compelled him to sell the scrunchies, toe rings, and nose-
hair clippers of all the semifamous people he's ever worked
with."

Uncle Ross shook his head and clucked. "Dirty,
shoplifting boy."

"You're telling me. But you know what? I think he's
way too much of a good guy at heart to be behind The 'Bu-
hoo.'"

"That's a disappointment. He was beginning to seem
interesting to me. What about that Italian stud, Rocco? The
one related to those delightful Belluccis? I bet there are
some skeletons in *their* closet. Or that blue-eyed surfer boy,
Trent? I *loved* him in *Emo Surfer*. So much emotion, so much
surfing . . ."

"Well, Rocco certainly has the smarts—but he's not
the least bit concerned with all that gossip stuff. Trent, bless
his blond heart, can barely string a sentence together to
talk—let alone write one out on a page, so I don't think he's
a prime candidate."

"Want about that delightful scamp, Anushka?"

"Well, she'd be a good candidate, but she's pretty
much out of the loop now that she's at Pomona Tech.
Besides, her ADHD is so bad I can't imagine her having the
patience to keep up a blog. Tanya's the only other one. But

she's like Trent—not about to split any atoms anytime soon, if you catch my drift."

"Dumb as a yoga mat?"

"You didn't hear it from me." Corliss's mind was now racing. "Of course it could be someone on the production end of things . . . the entire crew . . . all Max's assistants . . . the hair and wardrobe people . . ." Corliss took a piece of paper from her bag. "This is the call sheet. It has everyone's name on it from Michael Rothstein on down."

"Let me see that a moment."

Corliss handed it over. Uncle Ross took out his Michael Kors reading glasses, and as he looked down at the call sheet, he clutched his Turnbull & Asser tie. A small, choked sound escaped from his mouth.

"What is it, Uncle Ross? You're as white as your Vivienne Westwood boots."

Uncle Ross shuddered. "It's this name . . . *here*." He pointed to the call sheet and handed it to Corliss like it was infested with the West Nile virus.

Corliss looked at the name he'd pointed to. "Mingmei Rothstein? Michael Rothstein's wife?"

Uncle Ross nodded and bit his lip.

"What about her?"

Uncle Ross finished off his wine and held his glass aloft so the waitress could see. "I knew her as Mingmei Jin. But a few years ago I read in *Variety* that she'd married mega-mogul Michael Rothstein. You now know her as Mingmei *Rothstein*, but when she was Mingmei *Jin* she was my . . ."

"What? She was your what?"

"Prom date!"

"*What?*"

"It's true. She broke my heart, Corliss."

"*You went to your prom with Mingmei Rothstein?*" Corliss thought her head was going to explode.

"Please don't shout, Corliss. I was young. I was beautiful. Mingmei tracked me like she was hunting prey."

"But—but—I thought women were 'a vague blur' to you!"

"Well, they are now that Jurgen is my life partner. I cherish that—even though I just slipped the busboy my phone number."

"Classy."

"Corliss, don't judge. I have a complicated heart. And at one time it was full of nothing but Mingmei."

Corliss literally shook her head so that this information would settle inside it.

"She tore me into a million pieces, Corliss. She is a dangerous character and not to be trusted! If you're looking for someone behind that hateful blog, my money is on Mingmei!"

Corliss's mind was a blur. She couldn't believe Uncle Ross had some zany prom past with Mingmei Rothstein. But she *didn't* have trouble thinking of Mingmei as the person behind The 'Bu-hoo. Mingmei was just the kind of nutcase capable of such a thing. As their pizzas were delivered to the table, Corliss made a mental note to follow up on Uncle Ross's tip as soon as possible.

"Enjoy your food," said the waitress with a forced smile on her face. "Do you have any questions?"

"Yes," said Corliss, staring forlornly at the unidentifiable pizza in front of her. "Whatever happened to pepperoni?"

Five

Malibu Beach—10:17 A.M., the Next Morning

It wasn't even noon and Max was already at the end of his rope. His assistants fanned out behind him, matching his tense expression, and the camera crew waited until he could restore order. "Tanya!"

Tanya turned. "Max, whenever you raise your voice it goes all girly." She seemed to think this was funny.

Max counted to ten silently—and made a mental note to make the next words from his mouth come out in a manly whisper. "Yes, I am aware of that, Tanya. My Scientology counselor is trying to 'clear' my higher register. But that has nothing to do with the disruptions you've been causing. Now please apologize to JB. I will not let the morale of this production sink any deeper than it already has."

Tanya huffed and puffed and tossed her hair around to show how disgusted she was by having to apologize. "I'm sorry, JB."

Max rolled his fingers for her to continue. "For . . . ?"

Tanya sighed theatrically and rolled her eyes and tossed her hair around again. Max's assistants rolled their fingers. "Okay, all right!" Tanya turned to JB. "I'm sorry, JB, for handing you the two Band-Aids I was using to keep my nipples flat in this scene so you could sell them on eBay." She turned back to Max. "Is that okay?"

JB looked like he was about to die.

"Thank you, Tanya, that was very nice. And JB, do you accept her apology?"

JB nodded.

"Perfect. Now give Tanya back her nipple Band-Aids."

JB did as he was told. Tanya made a face when she looked down at them, all crumpled and sweaty from being balled up in JB's hands.

"Okay, I'm going to need some new nipple Band-Aids, please," she said to the nearest production assistant, who promptly ran off to fetch them.

Max wiped his brow and sent up a silent prayer to L. Ron Hubbard, founder of Scientology, that the second 'Bu episode would not be as brutally difficult as the pilot. "Great. Now that that's finished, I want everyone in their places, please."

The camera crew got back into place. The actors hit their marks. "Okay—and for the sixth time—in this scene I need the three of you to—" Max looked around. There were only *two* actors present. "Okay, where is Trent, please?" Trent was nowhere to be seen. Max's assistants dispersed like convicts set free, running up and down the beach looking for the missing surfer dude.

"I don't know where he could have gone," said Tanya, twirling her hair and looking scrumptious in a pink bebe bikini.

"He was just here trying to make me feel guilty for hanging out with Rocco. Which is totally not Trent's business since we're not, like, going out anymore. He's not the boss of my love life!"

"You and Rocco 'hanging out'?" said JB skeptically. "That's news to the Jeebster."

"Maybe we are and maybe we aren't. The point is it's nobody's business except mine and Rocco's. And, of course, Jesus's."

Max felt a vein pulse between his eyes. Several of his assistants returned, with Trent in tow. Maple syrup dripped from his big lips and what looked like bits of blueberry pancake were gathered at the top of his bathing suit.

"Trent!" Max shouted, all girly again. "Trent . . ." he repeated, but in his lower register. "Where have you been?"

Trent shuffled his feet and said, "Nowhere."

"Nowhere? There are bits of high-carb food all over you."

"No, there's not."

"Totally there is," said Tanya.

Max couldn't believe it. "Were you eating pancakes?"

Trent shook his blond head vigorously.

"I think you were, eating disorder dude," grinned JB. "You look like happy hour at IHOP."

Everyone was staring at Trent. He shuffled his feet again and avoided Max's eyes. "Uh, well, see, I tripped at the catering table and fell over, like, splat into this stack of, like, ten blueberry pancakes. And they were, like, all slathered in butter and syrup so they got stuck to me."

JB stifled a giggle. Max shot him a look.

Tanya scrunched up her face. "That is story, Trent. No one falls over splat into a sta unless he's, like, drooling over them in the firs

Max stepped between them. "Tanya, please, I'll handle this."

JB raised his hand. "Max, much as I'd love to stay here and grill Trent on his diet—*grill*, get it?—can I hit the little boys' room? I drank three Arnold Palmers before we set up and my back teeth are floating."

Max made a note on his iPhone to refill his antianxiety prescription. "Yes, JB, but please be quick about it. We are already two hours behind schedule."

"I'm a quick pee, you'll see!" JB ran off.

"Trent," said Max in his most paternal voice. "Didn't we have a good long talk about your diet and how important it is for you to stay far away from any foods that might make you gross and unappealing to the average television viewer?"

"Max, I swear I fell over onto the pancakes!" Trent turned to Tanya and frowned. Tanya tossed her hair around again and turned to Max. "Max," she said, looking over at Trent and shaking her head. "I'm sorry, but I can't do this scene."

"What?! Why?"

"Because I read that book, *The Secret*. Did you ever read that?"

"Tanya," said Max, exhaling loudly, "You are stepping very close to my last good nerve. I am trying to shame Trent into staying thin by humiliating him publicly. That always worked for me when my mother did it. Her endless carping— 'No one wants someone shaped like an igloo as a friend!'— she'd screech as I reached for my third Ho Ho."

"You like Ho Hos, too?" asked Trent hopefully.

Tanya looked at her nails. "Max, as Corliss would say, 'I think you've wandered a little off topic.'"

"Right," Max said, mortified that someone as dense as Tanya would notice such a thing. "What I meant to say was: What does *The Secret* have to do with you being able to do this scene?"

"'Cause in *The Secret* they say don't look at fat people if you want to stay thin." Tanya looked at Trent. Trent's lower lip started to quiver.

JB ran back, tying up his bathing suit. "Told you I was a quick pee!"

"JB," said Max, "take the pee talk way down. I don't discuss bodily functions openly." He turned to Tanya, focused, and tried to speak to her as if she had a normal brain capacity. "Tanya, I don't see what this scene has to do with fat people."

"God, Max, do I have to spell it out for you?" Tanya nodded over to Trent as if he weren't there. "Fatty McChicken Nuggets over here."

"Wow," said JB, "the plot thickens!"

"It's not the plot that's thickening, JB," yelped Tanya, who then continued in a whisper. "It's Trent's tummy."

But everyone heard Tanya's whisper. And then everybody looked at Trent's tummy. It was as flat as an ironing board.

"My tummy is fine, Tans! In fact, it's awesome." He punched himself there to show just how awesome it was. A few of Max's assistants applauded.

"Trent, I told you before, don't call me 'Tans!' That nickname is only for Anushka, my friend and former acting coach! She's the only one who can call me 'Tans'!"

Max looked to the heavens. "Tanya, *never, never, NEVER* say that person's name in my presence. And, as everyone can see, Trent's waistline is as tight as a steel drum."

"Maybe it is *now*," she said, "but whatever you eat shows up on your body two days later. That's a biological fact, according to *Teen People*. And the schedule says that we're filming this scene over the next two days, and I just want to be playing it with *Trent*, not Fatty Fatty Two By Four Can't Fit Through the Kitchen Door."

Trent looked at Max and pouted. "Is that another actor you've hired?"

Max took deep breaths and then got in a downward dog yoga position, with his butt in the air and his face toward the sand. "Okay, everyone, listen up. I am in this downward dog yoga position because I have run out of my antianxiety medication, and you are all pushing my crazy buttons."

JB nudged Tanya. "At least I'm no longer in the spotlight."

"Ow," said Tanya, "your elbows are bony, JB!"

"Silence, people!" said Max, still in his downward dog. "We are going to start this scene *now*. Tanya, you will look at Trent in the scene. He is not fat—only in danger of becoming so. JB, you will look at Tanya, who will be looking at Trent, who *is not fat*. Trent, you will remain, to the best of your ability, *not fat*. Where are my assistants? Can you please join me in the downward dog position?"

Max's assistants stepped forward and bent over with their butts in the air. "Thank you for your yoga solidarity. Here is what I need: Rocco standing by for his entrance, and Corliss on set ASAP."

The assistants stood up and ran off to get Corliss. Max stood up, too, feeling refreshed after his downward dog. A couple of the PAs brought Rocco to the set. He looked even bigger than usual, wearing painted-on red Andrew Christian lifeguard shorts and a tight-as-Saran-Wrap Calvin Klein mesh T-shirt. Veins bulged in his arms and his hands looked as big as catchers' mitts.

"Welcome to the set, Rocco, you're looking very, um, strong today," said Max.

"*Really* strong," said Tanya, looking him up and down with wide, appreciative eyes.

Rocco stared at Max a moment before saying, "I've been on the set for the last three hours, Max. Waiting in my trailer. Pouring over the mediocre bit of text that you call a script."

Max ignored this. "How nice for you. Now please stand just off camera and I will give you your cue."

Rocco fell to the sand where he proceeded to do a hundred military push-ups. Tanya counted all of them with her fingers.

"Wow," said JB, "don't break anything, Rocs."

Trent's upper lip curled at the sight of Rocco's display of brawn. "Shouldn't you be, like, all up in some library reading, like, something?"

Rocco continued his push-ups, but now with one hand. "Anyone who knows me knows I've always subscribed to the belief that one needs to have a sound mind *and* body."

Tanya let a giggle escape. "Looks like a sound body to me." She then crossed herself, kissed her crucifix necklace, and looked away.

"Where is Corliss?" Max shouted as loud as he could

without going up into his girly register. "I need Corliss!"

"I'm here, Max." She was coming up behind him. Max turned to look—and his heart stopped. Mingmei Rothstein was at her side.

"Hello, Max, darling," said Mingmei, extending her hand for him to kiss. Max wiped the sweat from his upper lip and did so. "*Enchanté*, as always. I do so love the charm of entertainment people."

"Hello, Mrs. Rothstein," Max said in his tiniest voice.

"Please, let's dispense with the formalities," she said, raising her *other* hand so that it might be kissed as well. "I tell everyone to call me 'Mingmei.' I've even instructed your delightful little lesbian assistant to call me 'Mingmei.'" She looked at Corliss.

"That's me," said Corliss, clearly exasperated, "a delightful little lesbian assistant!"

"It is?" said Tanya, looking startled.

"I sure hope it is," said JB, raising an eyebrow.

"Please, everyone," said Max uneasily, "welcome Mingmei here to our set."

Everyone made dutiful little waves as Mingmei dipped like the Queen of England, turning her nose in the direction of the makeup person. The makeup person promptly powdered it.

Mingmei was striking in her vintage Pucci wrap dress and ginormous Dita blackout glasses—and Max was in a blind panic about what her presence on the set might mean. "What is *she* doing here?" he said to Corliss after steering her out of earshot from everybody.

"I have no idea, Max. I was inside your trailer cross-referencing all the possible MBK suspects I have so far with their whereabouts at the time of the worst 'Bu-hoo blog entries when out of nowhere Mingmei just showed up."

Inside Max's head there was a big crashing sound, as if a hundred plates had just fallen off a high shelf. "But, Corliss? People like Mingmei don't just 'show up.' They are sent as *spies*. They are on *illicit missions* to undo me! They are agents from the network dispatched to see what I'm up to!"

"Max, the paranoia you display is pretty profound. I could recommend a shrink if you'd like."

"Please, Corliss. Scientologists don't believe in shrinks— or in Xanax for that matter. I'm cheating a little bit on that one. Don't sell me out."

"Max, Max, calm down. Mingmei isn't here as a spy for the network. She's not even the author of the blog. Uncle Ross had this theory that maybe she was—which I was all like, 'Are you for real?' about. But I've checked her background thoroughly and even interrogated her myself. She thinks a *blog* is something you inject in your lips! She did say something about being in one of the scenes we're shooting today, though. But that can't be right. Can it?"

"Oh, God . . ." Max knew it *was* right. The last time he'd seen Mingmei he'd said something like, 'Come to the set any day you want, Mingmei, and we'll put you in a scene.' He'd meant it as cocktail chatter—he'd been three mojitos down. He never thought she'd actually take him up on it.

"Listen, Corliss, I can explain the whole thing later," said Max, looking over to Mingmei, who was now being fanned by three of his assistants. "In the meantime, we have to figure something out."

"What is it?"

"Exactly what a middle-aged woman in a Pucci dress with enough face work to make herself look like an android would be doing on a beach with teenagers."

Corliss nodded across the beach to where Petey and the writers were huddled like a gaggle of black crows. "Do you want me to help brainstorm some ideas with them?"

"No, thank you, Corliss. I'll deal with them. What I need you to do is to continue to focus on the hunt for MBK. Morale on the set is at an all-time low, and it's because of that blog! We have to figure out who's writing it and expose that person to the world—or at least to *Entertainment Tonight*. I'm convinced it's someone on this very set. He or she or *it* knows too much. Your powers of observation are exceptional, and your instincts uncanny. I want you to keep close to me and watch. Not too close, of course, you know I have personal space issues. But if anyone says anything suspicious, I want you to follow up with questioning. Discreetly, of course."

"Don't worry, Max, discretion is my middle name."

"I thought it was 'Beverly'?"

Corliss exhaled and shook her head. "I'm *so* sorry I ever let that slip. But don't worry, Max. We'll find out who MBK is."

"What will I do without you, Corliss?"

"I'm not leaving for college just yet. Come on, let's get back to work."

Max nodded and he and Corliss headed over to Petey and the writers. As they did, Rocco stepped between them.

"What exactly is going on here, Max? My call was three

hours ago and I haven't been in front of a camera yet."

"You've been in your trailer the entire time?" said Corliss inquisitively.

"Excuse me?" said Rocco, looking at her strangely. "Yes, I have been in my trailer the entire time waiting to be called to the set and—"

"Rocco, please," Max said, trying to swat him away like a fly, "at the moment I have Mingmei Rothstein up my butt."

"Yoo-hoo," trilled Mingmei from a few yards off. "I'm ready for my close-up, Max!"

"One moment, Mingmei," said Max, trying to smile through his agony. He turned and headed toward the writers again. But once again, Rocco got in his way. "Excuse me, Rocco, I need to get by."

But Rocco wasn't going anywhere. "Rocco, seriously," said Corliss. "We'll only lose more time. Or is that your goal? Disrupting the set so you can have more time in your trailer? Do you keep a journal, by the way?"

Rocco stared at her incredulously. "What's with the cryptic line of questioning, Corliss? My only goal is to work."

"Waiting is part of work, Rocco," said Max.

"Waiting is part of waiting!" snarled Rocco.

"Okay, everyone," said Corliss, putting herself between the two men. "Let's just calm down. It's very hot today, and we're all backed up time-wise, and tempers can become inflamed, and people can get a little . . . inflammatory." She looked at Rocco nervously. "Especially when someone with hands the size of catchers' mitts is standing over them looking like he's ready to pounce."

Max moved close to Corliss. "Rocco *does* look a

little ferocious at the moment . . ."

Rocco's eyes narrowed. "I am not ready *to pounce*, as you so eloquently put it. I am merely trying to advocate for some professional behavior for once!"

Max clung to Corliss. Rocco's eyes were bulging, bloodshot. "Take it easy, Rocco," said Corliss, looking more than a little scared herself. "We're going to start right now, aren't we, Max?"

But Max was too frightened to respond. Something about Rocco said, "This is a man teetering on the edge."

"Well," said Rocco, moving his face close to Max's, "are we going to start OR WHAT??"

Max heard his teeth clack together. He tried to respond, but his throat was locked. He shook in his Gucci loafers and sputtered and blinked. He could only watch helplessly when Rocco stormed over to the camerawoman and thundered, "Since I'm not getting an answer—EVERYONE IN THEIR PLACES!"

"What are you doing?" Max finally squeaked out.

"I'm taking over."

Everyone froze, terrified.

"NOW!"

Tanya finally wriggled to her mark. JB did, too. "But, Rocs, how can you take over when you're *in* the scene?"

With that, Rocco let out a sound like a lion on the attack and knocked over the camera, which fell against a light tree, sending sparks flying. People scattered. Max let out a girly yelp and then checked his Zegna shorts to make sure there were no burn holes. Rocco ran off, growling and shaking his fists in the air. When he was gone and all was quiet, the camerawoman stepped forward and looked at the camera.

"Is anything wrong?" asked Max.

"It's broken. We'll have to call the studio and get a new one sent out. Might take a few hours, though."

Max knew his prayer to L. Ron Hubbard hadn't worked; the second episode was turning out to be a disaster—and surely news of that would sooner or later show up on The 'Buhoo. He also knew he had to do something immediately to show he was in charge, not only to the person who might be MBK, but also to his producer's wife, Mingmei Rothstein, who was giving him a very snotty look. "If the camera is broken," Max proclaimed, "then all the writers are fired!"

"But Max!" protested Corliss.

Petey shook his head. The writers slumped farther down than usual.

"Obviously, the scene we have been trying to shoot all morning was not good! And it was *so* not good that I had trouble knowing how to shoot it, which caused a slowdown in the process, which rightfully enraged one of our actors. It also was a scene that couldn't possibly have done justice to the enormously talented Mingmei Rothstein!"

"Why, Max," cooed Mingmei, no longer looking snotty, "that's so sweet of you to say!"

Max knew the tactic was working. "I repeat," he said, pointing one manicured cuticle in the air. "All the writers are fired."

"Except for me, Max," droned Petey. "You'll recall my contract says you can't fire me."

Mingmei looked at Max like, "Who is this schmuck?"

"That's true, Petey," said Max. "But your contract does

stipulate that I can reassign you to hair and makeup if I so choose. Would you like that?"

Petey shook his head vigorously.

"Fine then. Back to the writers' trailer. You are to return with a script worth shooting."

Petey slunk off. Mingmei sidled up to Max. "That was a very powerful display of authority, Max."

"Thank you, Mingmei."

"It kinda made me happy in my Pucci, if you catch my meaning."

Max understood her only too well. Mingmei was coming on to him! "Thank you, Mingmei, that's, um, very flattering. But your husband is my boss and—"

"What does that have to do with anything, you delicious man of power?" she said as she ran taupe-colored fingernails all around his ears.

"It's just—" That's when Max felt a tugging at his shorts. He looked down. It was Legend. "Hey, Maxth. Can I borrow the keyth to your car? Rocco sayth he'th outta here and he wanth thomeone to drive him to Muthcle Beach."

Somewhere in the Woods of Holly—Later that Day

Dear 'Bu-sters—

Yeeeeeouch, it's been a tough week for M2!
Poor guy can't catch a break. His producer's wife
is coming on to him (BLECH), his number one
assistant Clueless Meyers is about to take off for
college (HOORAY!), and his stars are staging an
insurrection (WOULDN'T YOU?). But that's not his
biggest problem.

Not by a long shot, *'Bu*-babies.

It's Rocco DiTullio, smoldering Italian Stallion,
brainiac weight lifter, Bellucci cousin, and would-
be director.

Now I want everyone to sit down before I go
any further and take a deep breath. Because
this thing is big. Bigger than JB's goofball eBay
antics. Bigger than Trent's crazizzle Jenny Craig
revelation. Bigger than, well, Rocco's bulging
biceps.

In fact it's the *cause* of Rocco's bulging biceps.
Anyone? I'll give you a hint. Big muscles plus real
cranky attitude equals?

Yup, I bet some of you got it: *The dude's on steroids.*

CUE BABY SCREAMS: *WAH, WAH!!!!*

Oh, yeah. Rocs's got it bad and that ain't good. The well-read kid with the looks of a Michelangelo has a monkey on his back. And it's one of those really mean monkeys that bites and spits! His body muscle mass has increased by almost twenty percent, but now he's HOOKED. Do ya think the virginal Tanya Ventura will keep chasing his rock hard butt once she finds this out? Maybe she'll go back to Trent, who's fer shizzle waiting for her, and chewing on a pack of Twizzlers while he's doin' it!

Boy, is this one dysfunctional crew OR WHAT?

Seems Rocco broke that camera because he was all hopped up on 'roids! A little sumthin' they call 'roid rage. And there's nuttin' they can do for ya. Except lock you away somewhere and take away your 'roids!

M2 is trying to keep this all hush-hush. *The 'Bu* pilot airs next week, and he's got to get the second show in the can before then. The UBC network's publicity machine is on overdrive, and Goth Roth's giant hairy head will pop off if there are any more bad revelations about the cast!

But I can't help myself!!! MBK has to reveal and reveal! It's not that I don't want *The 'Bu* to be a big, freakin' hit. I just want to bring the dirt, too!

In closing, dear *'Bu*-licous *'Bu*-bunnies, what's going on with that delightful little minx Anushka Peters? It's been a little too quiet over in her corner of the world.

Maybe she's lying facedown in a punch bowl? Or maybe she's actually studying?? LMAO! Sure, we've all seen those paparazzi shots of Anushka on the Pomona Tech campus looking all studious. Walking around with her book bag, sitting in the quad. But come on! Does anyone believe those pix???? Fact is, it isn't like Ms. Peters to be off radar for so long. Why does MBK think she might be planning another surprise attack on her former

'Bu colleagues? Say, something big right before the pilot airs next week?

I's just sayin'!

Just remember: You can round up these starlets, take away their drink tickets, and dump their sorry butts at Wilmer Valderrama's bachelor pad, but you can't keep 'em from getting the attention they demand!

Yours in *'Bu*-ty-liciousness,
MBK

Six

Michael Rothstein's Home Gym—a Few Days Later, 6:27 A.M.

"Thanks for coming out so early, Max," said Michael Rothstein as a gorgeous Yogalates instructor twisted him into a pretzel shape. "And you, too, Corliss. Max is constantly singing your praises."

"It's my pleasure, Mr. Rothstein," said Corliss, stifling a yawn.

"Corliss and I were happy to come over before the crack of dawn," said Max, whose head throbbed from getting up so early. It didn't help matters that Michael Rothstein was dressed in a kind of chartreuse wrestler's Onesie that made him look like a hairy, lime-green beach ball.

"Like this get-up? Shows all my nooks and crannies!" Michael patted his fat stomach as the gorgeous Yogalates instructor smiled and twisted him into another complicated position.

"It's very stylish, Mr. Rothstein," said Corliss, stifling another yawn.

"I had no idea you were so limber, Michael," Max added, knowing he had to compliment the portly producer, who looked like he was in tremendous pain.

"Can't believe I can put my feet near my ears, can ya?"

"It's impressive, Michael, that your feet are even anywhere *near* your ears." Michael's eyes were bulging out of his head, and his forehead was purple from exertion. Max and Corliss looked away.

"Yeah, well, Quinoa here says if I'm patient I'll soon be able to stick my head entirely up my ass." Quinoa, a beautiful young woman dressed in a blindingly white leotard, smiled serenely. "That's a joke. You two look so serious."

"Sorry," said Max, smiling and nudging Corliss to do the same. "Ha ha. That's funny."

Max knew his laugh came off as completely fake. He couldn't help it. He was terror-stricken about what this little impromptu meeting meant. He'd only been called about it the night before while he was lounging poolside at the Mondrian. Seven leggy models were surrounding him as he told them how humble he felt to be the creator/director of what would surely be the next biggest thing on TV. His one moment of serenity in weeks of turmoil had then been interrupted by Michael Rothstein's assistant calling to say Max was to report to Michael's home in the Hollywood Hills for "reasons that will be specified once there." That's why he'd brought Corliss—he was too frightened to face Michael Rothstein on his own.

"So, um, Michael. I was wondering about this, um, 'reasons that will be specified once there' thing that your assistant said on the phone last night."

"Pah," Michael said, "don't mind him. He's so *dramatic*."

Max heaved an internal sigh of relief. Corliss gave him a quick thumbs-up. Maybe Mingmei *hadn't* told Michael about her crush on him. Maybe the writers he'd just fired *didn't* report him to the Writers Guild again. Maybe Michael *hadn't* been reading The 'Bu-hoo like half of America.

"Of course," said Michael ominously. "There is one weensy little problem." Quinoa now had Michael tied up to several ropes that came out of the walls. He looked like an enormous chartreuse spider caught in a web.

Max gulped. "There is?"

"Well . . . let's just put it this way: I got a call last night from the Bellucci family lawyer. Any idea why?"

Max felt his chest tighten. "Well, um, Michael," Max said, stalling. "Rocco did have a rather inappropriate moment on the set this week." Max started to get hot under the collar. "He, uh, broke some camera equipment because of a little, tiny artistic disagreement we had." He could tell Michael was skeptical. "But that was resolved internally, and I hardly think there's any need to get lawyers involved."

"Screw the lawyers. The kid's in Sicily. *That's* the problem."

"Sicily!" shouted Corliss.

Max didn't understand. "You mean Rocco's on vacation? But we're in the middle of taping the second episode!"

"Not on vacation, you *schmuck*," growled Michael as Quinoa put her foot in the small of his back and pressed as hard as she could.

"If not vacation, then what? I certainly didn't authorize—"

"I know you didn't, Max," said Michael as Quinoa

dug her heels into his lower back. "Lighten up, Quinoa, I'm having some kidney distress this week. Can't go ten minutes without peeing. You keep pressing that hard and I might wet my Onesie."

Corliss winced. Quinoa smiled serenely, released her foot, and brought Michael some Agave-sweetened green tea.

"Thanks kid, take ten. I want to talk to these two kids alone."

Quinoa floated out of the room.

Max and Corliss looked at each other in disbelief. "I don't understand, Michael," said Max. "If he's not on vacation, what is Rocco doing in Sicily?"

"That's where one of his cousins is," said Michael, toweling off. "Runs a fancy treatment center."

"*Treatment center?*"

"Yup. Rocco's in 'roid rehab. His family put him there. Staged an intervention, the whole *megillah*."

"*'Roid rehab?*" Max's mind did loop-di-loops. Corliss's jaw dropped to the floor.

"Come on, Max, haven't you been reading The 'Bu-hoo?"

"Uh-oh," said Corliss.

"No, Michael, I haven't been reading The 'Bu-hoo! You'll forgive me for speaking forcefully, but I've told everyone on the show not to dignify that blog by reading it. How could I then go ahead and do so myself?"

"I'm not dignifying anything, but that's where I first heard of this Rocco 'roid business. Which turns out to be true! And weren't you supposed to be finding out who was writing that blog so we could hang him or her out to dry? I've got my lawyer on it in a big way, Max. I want to take that blog *down*."

Corliss stepped up. "Actually, Mr. Rothstein, I'm hard at work trying to determine who is behind The 'Bu-hoo. I have charts and files and reports. I've even created a database of clues."

"She's doing a wonderful job, Michael. We just don't know who this MBK person is. And I guess we also didn't know Rocco had a steroid problem."

"Max, the kid's the size of a sequoia and he pulverized one of our most expensive cameras. Maybe you shoulda done the math."

"But such a talent—and from such a good family!"

"Who gives a flying flip what family he's from? We got ourselves an actor who's missing in action."

Max's mind sped up. He saw the calamity in the near future. He certainly did the math now—and fast. "But we can't finish the second episode without Rocco and it's due this week!"

"Exactamundo, my friend," said Michael, draping a sweaty arm over Max's shoulder. "That's why I want that kid's Sicilian butt back here on these shores, pronto."

"But how, Michael? With all due respect, I can't just put Corliss on a plane to Sicily and have her bring him back. You know how powerful his family is. She wouldn't even get close to him!"

"I don't even have a passport!" Corliss yelped.

"Not my problem, kids," said Michael, patting two sweaty palms on their backs. "And have you ever noticed, Max, that your voice gets a little girly in the upper register?"

"Um, yes," said Max, lowering his voice. "I'm working

on that with Legend's speech coach."

"So you'll have Rocco back on set this week?" Michael was moving Max and Corliss toward the door.

"But I'd have to go through the Belluccis! Tell them Rocco shouldn't be in rehab now. Convince them a 'roid-addicted kid *on television* is better than a 'roid-free one in Sicily! I can't argue with them, Michael. I'd be blacklisted from the business."

Michael Rothstein frowned. "Again, not my problem. Our pilot airs three nights from tonight, and if it gets the ratings I think it's gonna get, we'll need Rocco here for publicity. *Access Hollywood! Entertainment Tonight! Extra!* Not to mention finishing that second episode so we can air it. We need that kid stateside, do you hear me?"

Max had no earthly idea how he was going to make this particular magic happen. He looked to Corliss for comfort, but she looked just as perplexed. "Corliss, please do me a favor and get my Porsche from Mr. Rothstein's valet. I'll be out in two seconds. We've got to back get to my trailer immediately and start brainstorming."

"Gotcha, Max. I'll have the engine running." Corliss flew out.

"Cute little patootie," said Michael as Corliss went. "By the way, Max, thanks for putting Mingmei in that scene. Took the burn off around here, if you know what I mean."

"Did I hear my name?" It was Mingmei, standing in the doorway wearing a translucent silk Dolce & Gabbana bathrobe, pink Ferragamo mules, and about two hundred Elsa Peretti bracelets.

"Speak of the devil," said Michael with a sneer.

Mingmei ignored her husband and offered her hands for Max to kiss. "Divine man, by consenting to direct me as a special guest star on *The 'Bu* you have opened up my creative center. Can you tell?" Mingmei stood back and opened her bathrobe to see if Max could tell. Underneath she was wearing an itty-bitty bikini that was an odd choice for a woman some people thought was crowding seventy.

"Close your bathrobe, Mingmei," said her husband with disgust. "No one wants to contemplate your creative center."

"Simmer down, hairball," said Mingmei, smiling through her teeth and closing her robe. "I want to bring up something to Max before he goes. It's about that *delicious* blog."

Oh, God, Max thought. *Here we go . . .*

"Perusing it is simply the favorite pastime of all my girlfriends. Of course we know half of it is lies, like all that business about how atrociously *awful* a director you are."

Max got queasy.

"But we can't stop reading it! All those terrible things your cast gets up to. Jail time, various addictions, messy romance—*so faboo.*"

"Get to the point, Mingmei," said Michael. "Max is a busy man."

"I will, sweatbag," said Mingmei, once again through her teeth. "The thing is, Max, your lesbian assistant told me you're trying to determine who's writing it."

"My who?"

Mingmei plowed on. "If that's the case, I just want to add my two cents."

"*Of course* you do," said Michael, staring her down.

"Well, you see, it occurs to me that every lesbian

"assistant I've ever met has not been trustworthy. Call me
prejudiced, but there's something about the combination of
lesbianism and assistantship that becomes toxic."

"Wait, do you mean *Corliss*?"

"Besides," Mingmei continued, "she has access to
simply everyone!"

Max shook his head. "I can assure you, Mingmei, that
Corliss is not the author of that blog."

"Keep an eye on her, Max," said Michael. "Mingmei may
be a collagen-enhanced harpy, but her instincts about people
are usually pretty faboo."

"Kiss, kiss, *Herr* Director," said Mingmei, twirling as she
exited the room, clanking her bracelets as she went. "Keep an
eye on that girl!"

Michael patted Max on the back and moved him toward
the door. "Hey, before you go, you want Quinoa to realign your
chakras? Really gives you a burst of perspective."

"Um, no thanks, Michael. Scientologists aren't allowed
to let other people touch their chakras without special
permission."

"Suit yourself," said Michael, giving Max a half-friendly
shove out the door. "Now get back to work. We got a pilot
premiere in three days at Grauman's Chinese Theatre. I want
The 'Bu house in order, you hear me? So find out where Rocco
is and who is writing that *farkakta* blog!"

Max's Porsche Boxster—Driving on the 405, Fifteen Minutes Later

"Okay, Corliss," said Max, driving a good twenty miles
over the speed limit, while guzzling a Starbucks Venti triple

espresso latte. "I think I have an idea about how to track down Rocco."

"Excellent, Max, because I'm stumped. So stumped, in fact, I was beginning to feel like a certain nickname a certain someone who shall remain nameless coined for me."

"Corliss," said Max, zooming in and out of lanes, "there is no time for hieroglyphics—speak plainly."

"I was beginning to feel *Clueless*! It's what MBK calls me in that stupid blog."

Max shuddered. "That is exactly why I cannot stand that blog. It makes my blood boil to hear untrue things. You are so far from clueless. You are, in fact, clue . . . full! Do you think there's another Starbucks between here and the beach?" he said, making an enormous sucking sound as he drained the last of his latte.

"Max, maybe you should go easy on that stuff. And thanks for the kind words, but I don't feel 'clue-full' at all about this Rocco situation. I wouldn't know where to begin. Italy isn't exactly my hang." Corliss looked up ahead as the exits flipped by. "By the way, if you don't make the next exit, we're going to end up in San Francisco."

Max turned hard, his tires screeching, and made the exit. Corliss closed her eyes and prayed. When she opened them, she could see Max gripping the steering wheel so tightly his knuckles were white. Corliss was beginning to worry about his mental state. She'd seen his anxiety ramping up in the last few days, and had noted that neither Xanax nor his Scientology counselor had been much help. The early morning visit to Michael Rothstein's seemed to put Max even more dangerously close to the edge. "Max, maybe we should pull over and get some breakfast and wait for some of this rush hour traffic to break up."

"Listen Clueless—I mean *Corliss*—we can't slow down now. We have our work cut out for us today! First, I will focus on the Rocco situation. I know an Italian man who sells calzones at the Farmers' Market. He has a very thick accent and he looks like something out of *The Sopranos*. He's always making remarks about all his powerful friends in the 'Old Country' and how if I ever needed any *favors* he'd be happy to help out."

"Max, that sounds totally dangerous. And weird. A calzone salesman with mob ties?"

"No one said 'mob,' Corliss, please. He's just *connected*. He should be able to break through the Bellucci curtain."

"Okay, Max, but be careful."

"Don't worry about me, Corliss. *You* worry about who is writing that blog. I want you to spend these next few days before *The 'Bu* premiere living, eating, and breathing the search for MBK. Do we understand each other?"

"Yes, Max, but—"

"But *what*, Corliss? I'm flying over an emotional no-fly zone at the moment and I wish you'd say what's on your mind. We don't have time to mince words, hem and haw, beat around the bush, et cetera. What is it?" As he said this, his Porsche Boxster, his baby, the light of his life and the sunshine of his existence, sputtered to a stop.

Corliss felt his pain. "I was just going to say I thought the gas gauge looked a little low."

Malibu Beach—*The 'Bu* Catering Tent—8:32 A.M.

Corliss adjusted her Tommy Girl sunglasses. She wasn't good at lying, and she wanted to make sure Trent didn't see her eyes as she grilled him about The 'Bu-hoo. She knew, of course, that there was no way he was capable of writing the blog, but it had occurred to her (when she and Max were being towed off the 405) that maybe Trent was telling some of his friends inside stories about *The 'Bu*. He was connected to a lot of young Hollywood-types because of *Emo Surfer*, to say nothing of his friendships with real surfers up and down the California coast. This made Corliss suspicious; Uncle Ross had told her never to trust surfers soon after he had to fire one who was his pool boy.

Trent was seated at a picnic table in the far corner of the tent. Corliss approached him, trying to appear as nonchalant as possible. He was staring forlornly at a salad topped with sprouts. "Hey, Trent. Looks like some healthy eats."

Trent pouted and shook a packet of Brewer's Yeast all over his salad. "Yeah, I'm *totally* off the Jenny now because I *totally* couldn't stick to it. This is a breakfast salad Max's Ayurveda coached FedExed to me. If I eat it all I can have a bowl of lentils for lunch." He looked like he was about to cry.

"Wow, you really are committed to staying in shape. I know how hard it is to keep to a diet. I crave fried Snickers all the time, but do you see me scarfing them?" Corliss shook her head. "No way." She felt she had to make sure Trent related to her in order to gain his confidence. "Mind if I take a seat?" He shook his blond head.

"So, Trent," Corliss said, pretending to make small talk, "just how much would you say you talk about what goes on at

The 'Bu with people not associated with the show? Surfers, say?"

"Um, I dunno. Like, not at all?"

"Not at all? Are you serious? What about your Hollywood friends? You've been in show business for a few years now. You're always hanging out with some fabulous somebody or other. Don't you ever shoot the breeze with them about what goes on here? Max's meltdowns? Tanya's tizzies? JB's . . . JB-ness?"

"Corliss, first of all, surfers don't care about TV shows. And I'm, like, a fake surfer anyway. I just kinda do it for the tan." He pulled down his Billabong board shorts to show an inch of solid whiteness below his golden-brown abs.

"Wow," said Corliss, suddenly feeling light-headed, "I forgot about your tan."

"And, like, second, I don't hang out with Hollywood types anymore, ever since Tanya and I broke up. Whenever I do, she's always there, getting more fake by the minute. Which, like, totally bums me out."

"Hmmm, very interesting. So Trent Owen Michaels isn't the player The 'Bu-hoo seems to suggest you are?"

"What, that blog? Whatevs, Corliss. I don't read that junk. I'm surprised you do."

"Me? I don't read it either, Trent. Blech, I never liked gossip. And, irony of ironies, here I am in L.A., the gossip kingdom of the world! In fact, we might be the only two people who *don't* read that blog." He looked at her with his big, blue puppy dog eyes. She knew he was telling the truth, and she felt she could come clean with him. "Just between you and me," she said, moving closer to him and lowering her shades, "I'm trying to figure out who's writing The 'Bu-hoo because that person is causing a lot of trouble."

"Well, good luck. If I hear anything, I'll let you know. I don't know a lot of people who write, so I don't think I'll be a big help. By the way, you look totally babelini today," he said with a little smile. "That's surfer for poppin'."

"Thanks," said Corliss, blushing. "You look pretty babelini yourself, Trent." Now totally red-faced, she leaped from the picnic table and headed off to interrogate her next suspect. She fanned herself as she went. Trent was not at all her type, but still, whenever she got close to him, she couldn't help but be *impressed*.

"Corliss?" called Trent. "There *is* one thing you should know."

Corliss turned back. "There is?" Trent had a very serious look on his face and she'd *never* seen Trent with a serious look on his face. In an instant Corliss became convinced Trent was going to finally divulge something that would help her unlock the MBK mystery. She scrambled over to him and leaned in very close so he could whisper whatever crucial information he was about to convey. "You can trust me, Trent. What is it?"

"It just occurred to me when you stood up and walked away . . ." He seemed torn, afraid to say what he had to say.

"Yes, Trent. Is it helpful information?"

"Kinda."

"I'm all ears. And remember: This is *just between you and me*."

"Okay, Corliss. I think you'll want it that way, anyway." Trent took a big gulp of air and then let it out. "You have Brewer's Yeast all over your butt."

Hair and Makeup Trailer—9:53 A.M.

Corliss looked at her watch. Tanya had been sitting in the makeup chair for over forty minutes, and yet hardly any makeup had been applied to her face. Darby, the makeup technician, was just staring at her, making "Hmmm" sounds. Corliss thought she was going to lose her mind. "Tanya, can't I just ask you a few questions while you're sitting in the chair?"

"Corliss, I told you," said Tanya. "Darby has to have absolute silence when he's working on my face. Because my face is like his—what's that word for what artists paint on?"

"Canvas?" supplied Corliss.

"Yeah, I think so. My face is like his *canvas*. And he needs to be—what's that word for when artists have ideas?"

"Inspired?" offered Corliss.

"That sounds right."

"Okay, I'll make you a deal, Tanya. If I can just have five minutes of your time, I promise to get you as many tickets to the premiere as you want."

"Seriously! Because all my cousins are coming in from New York and that would be so, so awesome if they didn't have to watch the show from their motel."

"You're putting them up at a motel? Isn't that kinda cheap?"

"Corliss, I come from a good Catholic family that doesn't believe in birth control. I have forty-seven cousins! I can't put them up at the Chateau Marmont. I would spend my whole paycheck for the season."

Corliss gulped. "So you need forty-seven tickets to the premiere?"

"Uh-huh," said Tanya, pondering Darby, who was

pondering her face. "Do we still have a deal?"

"Well," Corliss said weakly. "I think I can get them into the *party* at least."

Tanya tossed her luxurious brown locks and thought about it. "Okay, Corliss, it's a deal. Forty-seven tickets under the name 'Ventura' to the premiere party. Darby, can you leave us alone for five minutes?" Darby pouted and left. "Okay, Corliss, what do you want to talk about?"

Corliss had to be careful. Tanya wasn't the sharpest knife in the drawer, but sometimes she surprised Corliss with her observations. "Tanya, look, the thing is, it's just been so long since we caught up." Corliss hated herself for having to lie. But then she remembered her promise to Max to help reveal MBK. "I just wanted to check in with you about, you know, your hobbies, pastimes, your ability to concentrate long enough to keep a daily record of what goes on at *The 'Bu* . . ."

"Huh?"

Corliss saw suspicion etched on Tanya's face. She knew she had to backtrack. "No, I just thought, you know, you're becoming more popular in Hollywood. You're more on 'the scene' these days." Corliss made big quotation marks with her hands even though she'd emphasized *the scene* when she'd said it. "And, you know, there's a lot of 'buzz' about *The 'Bu* . . ." Corliss made quotation marks with her hands again.

"Corliss, what's wrong? You're being totally spastic with your hands."

"Sorry." Corliss realized she was confusing Tanya by making quotation marks with her hands. "I just, you know, imagine a lot of people ask you for gossip about, for instance, your relationship with Trent, what Max is *really* like as a director, why Anushka was really fired from the show, and—"

"Corliss! Stop right there." Tanya kissed her crucifix necklace and proceeded quietly. "Jesus says it's a sin to gossip. And I follow Jesus's path. And if Jesus says 'Ye Shalt Don't Gossip,' then you better believe I shalt don't, like, gossip."

Tanya's convoluted syntax always staggered Corliss. And a commandment for gossiping? That was a new one for Corliss. She'd gone to Sunday school as a kid, but she didn't have any recollection of gossip being mentioned in the Bible. But Tanya looked so sincere as she professed her gossip innocence. "Okay, Tanya. I hope I didn't insult you."

"You could never insult me, Corliss. We're like sisters. Except you're shorter and don't have a modeling contract with Revlon. Now can I call Darby back into the trailer? He has ADHD, and sometimes it's hard for him to refocus after he's been on a break reading *Men's Health* for too long."

"Sure, Tanya," said Corliss, satisfied once and for all that there was no way on Earth Tanya could organize her tiny brain enough to be the writer of The 'Bu-hoo. That left only one cast member for Corliss to interrogate. And she was dreading it.

JB's Trailer—10:26 A.M.

Corliss stood outside JB's trailer, trying to gather the courage to go in. She'd saved JB for last because even though in some ways he was the prime MBK suspect, she so didn't want to believe he was capable of causing so much trouble. Still, she had a job to do. She girded herself and knocked on his door. "JB, it's Corliss. I don't care what you're doing in there on your computer—unless it's totally gross—but I wanted to have a little chat."

JB opened the door with his patented big, goofy smile. "Look who it is! Corliss Meyers, soon to be Columbia University freshman. Sorry—fresh*woman*. What can I do you for?"

Corliss knew there was no way JB would put up with her amateur sleuthing—he was way too smart. She was just going to have to be completely honest with him and state her business, but without pulling any punches. She threw her shoulders back and took a breath. "I'm here on business, JB. May I come in?"

"*Entrez-vous, s'il vous plait*—which means 'Come on in, why doncha?' Although I can't be responsible for your personal safety once inside—bwa-ha-ha!" He made Dracula arms and bared his teeth.

Corliss rolled her eyes. JB might have been dropping bits of his geek act in the last few weeks, but there was still a *whole lot of it* in play. This seemed especially true once she stepped inside his trailer. The entire place was plastered with comic books, X-Men figurines, and posters of Brooke Burke in various bikinis. JB's computer was indeed on, but Corliss was relieved to see it open to a website that sold Accutane in bulk.

"Welcome to Geek Central, Cor. I've got to be on set in twenty minutes, but I'm all yours until then." He raised an eyebrow. "And I do mean *all yours*."

"Cut it out, JB, I'm here on serious business."

"Wow," he said. "Is everything okay? You do look serious."

"Everything's fine. And because I can't lie to you

because you're *almost* as smart as I am, I've decided to just come out and ask."

"Wow, this does sound serious. You've got your serious face on and everything."

Corliss made her serious face even more serious. She had to be tough with JB, or else he'd joke his way out of the discussion. She thought back to interrogation scenes she'd seen on TV shows like *Law & Order* and *Boston Legal*. JB was a friend, but right now he was a suspect. "JB, do you now or have you ever at any time had any connection to the person known as MBK?" JB opened his mouth to speak. "And I want the truth."

"Corliss, it's me, JB. Your best friend at *The 'Bu*. I could never lie to you."

"Then what is your answer?" She closed her eyes and prepared herself for the worst. JB had the intelligence, Internet know-how, and off-kilter perspective to be MBK. Of course, if he *was* MBK it would have to be the end of their friendship. Which would be one of the worst things to ever happen to Corliss. She waited for his answer, all balled up, but JB wasn't saying anything. She creaked her eyes open a little to see what was going on.

JB was looking at her so sweetly. "Of course I don't have anything to do with MBK or writing that blog."

"Phew, I'm so glad! Do you swear?"

"Cub Scouts honor."

"You haven't been in the Cub Scouts in years, JB. Look in me in the eye and tell me you aren't MBK."

"Corliss, I am a victim of that blog as much as anybody! Do you think I would have outed *myself* online as some creepy, day-trading teen who stole his costars' stuff to sell on eBay to get himself out of debt—especially when I *am* a creepy, day-trading teen who stole his costars' stuff to sell on eBay to get himself out of debt? Or *was,* I should say. I've paid off most of what I owe and haven't signed onto a day-trading website for two weeks, three days, and fourteen hours!"

"Congratulations, JB, but I don't know what truly lurks inside your weirdo heart. Maybe you outed yourself as a cry for help."

"Corliss," said JB, looking as serious as he'd ever looked. "I can assure you I was perfectly happy using my mother's credit cards to make thousands of dollars worth of bad stock trades online. It was the most fun I've ever had! Outside of the times I get to watch Darby do Tanya's makeup," he added dreamily.

"Boy, you say some really gay things sometimes, JB."

"I know! Even though I'm a 'ro not a 'mo! Another thing I'm not is MBK. And I'd swear on a stack of Lindsay Lohan rehab reports."

"Now *that* I believe." Corliss exhaled. She was satisfied. "I'm so sorry to even have to ask, JB. I just knew in my heart you had nothing to do with that blog, but you gotta admit you're smart enough, funny enough, observant enough, and techno-geek enough to be a prime suspect."

"Hmm, when you put in all the flattery, I see what you mean. But why the sad face? Aren't you happy I'm not MBK?"

"I'm completely happy about that—but completely *unhappy* I have to keep looking for MBK."

JB looked at his watch. "I'd love to help you out, but I gotta run. My next scene is up. The one where Tanya's character gets hypothermia and I have to roll her in a blanket until she gets warm. Fun times!"

"Oh, well," said Corliss, glancing at JB's computer. "Do you mind if I order some Accutane while I'm here?"

"Go crazy!" said JB, downing a breath mint and dashing out.

Seven

Grauman's Chinese Theatre—the Rooftop Party Deck—9:12 P.M., Three Days Later

"To *The 'Bu*," said Uncle Ross, holding a glass of champagne high in the air and waving it over Hollywood Boulevard, which sparkled below. "A palpable hit!"

Corliss gazed at everyone on the pagoda-peaked, Chinese lantern-strewn rooftop. It looked like Celeb Central. Christina Aguilera was chatting with Lauren Bush, who was standing next to Brody Jenner, who was feeding canapés to Jennifer Hudson. It seemed as if all of Hollywood had come out for the premiere of *The 'Bu*, which had just screened to tumultuous applause in the theater below.

Of course, *The 'Bu* cast was there, too, roped off in a little VIP area—and looking amazing. JB was working nerd chic in a serious way: Ted Baker slim-cut magenta trousers, a vintage powder-blue tuxedo shirt, and eggplant-colored Gucci loafers. And Trent, usually sporting tattered Aussie Beach Bum shorts, with hair working that electric socket look, had also completely pulled it together. His blond hair was slicked back over his ears, and he wore plum slacks, a white linen shirt (untucked), and a yellow and white woven Trina Turk jacket that made his ice-blue eyes pop.

The boys were, however, no match for Tanya, who looked more and more spectacular the longer she was in Los Angeles. She was living up to all the buzz that said she'd take the Most Devastating Girl on TV title from Anushka. She was draped in a pink-print Dior minidress, which she'd accented with a wide crocodile belt, towering Louboutin pumps, and Coach's new venomously chic snakeskin handbag.

Corliss felt drab by comparison. Then she caught sight of herself in one of the gigantic gilded mirrors that had been placed around the party—and she kind of liked what she saw. She was finally wearing the velvet Oscar de la Renta tiger dress that Uncle Ross had picked up for her at Barneys two months ago, and her new Pierre Hardy color-block heels were pretty stylin'. *Okay, so maybe I do look a little like Halloween on stilts. But in this crowd, that's a good thing!*

The entire scene, in fact, reminded Corliss of the nonstop glamour that was being a part of *The 'Bu. Of course it won't be nonstop once I leave L.A. to start school. It will, in fact, be stop-stop—and back to the books.* But for the moment, Corliss made the entire, perfect, dream-like scene freeze so she could brand it forever in her memory.

Then she came back to reality and something tugged inside her heart. In spite of the party's dazzling veneer, things weren't as perfect as they could have been. Anushka wasn't there, for one. She was off studying hard at Pomona Tech, or at least Corliss hoped she was. Several of Anushka's classmates had sold stories to the tabloids about how Anushka was never in class anymore, which worried Corliss. And she hadn't heard from her glamorous pal in over a week, even though she'd secretly sent her an invitation to the premiere. Corliss wasn't sure whether to believe the rumors or trust that her loose-cannon friend was finally getting her act together. Corliss had decided that the second option required much less emotional inner turmoil, so that's the one she was going with for now.

Rocco was still nowhere to be found. One rumor had him napping on the deck of P. Diddy's yacht somewhere off the coast of Sardinia. And, in spite of her protests, Max had gotten in touch with the old calzone salesman at the Farmers' Market. He was certainly willing to help track down Rocco—if Max would cut him in on some of his *'Bu* royalties. And give him the mortgage to his house. And place illegal bets on horses. Corliss had eventually talked Max out of all this. Somehow Max negotiating with old-school gangsters seemed to Corliss like a particularly gruesome Quentin Tarantino movie in the making.

The truth was, there was a lot of turmoil in *'Bu*-land if you knew enough to peek behind the fabulousness. Trent was still making sad surfer-puppy eyes at Tanya, who was tossing her hair at him and checking her iPhone every two minutes. And JB, who was still trying to get himself out of debt because of his online shenanigans, was as fidgety and nervous as ever.

To top off the less-than-perfect vibe, Corliss had yet to uncover the identity of MBK. She'd spent the last three days grilling the entire cast and crew, not to mention the UBC network executives. So many doors had been slammed in her face, her nose was sore. She was beginning to lose hope that they'd ever learn who was writing the hated blog. Her last crucial assignment for Max and it looked like she was going to blow it. Corliss was bummed—and she wasn't alone. None of *The 'Bu* kids seemed to be in the mood for partying. Corliss watched as they listlessly held their glasses in the air, joining Uncle Ross in his toast as he said, without a lot of energy, "To *The 'Bu*."

Finally, Max sidled up to Corliss. "The premiere went so brilliantly, but everyone looks so sad."

"Well, Max, all their secrets have been exposed online, two of them are in love with the wrong people, and if the show is as big a hit as the audience tonight seemed to think it is, this cast will *really* have to start working."

Max looked sad now, too. "I'm going to miss your shrewd insights, Corliss. They come out of left field and then hit me like an avalanche of snow at Telluride."

"And one more toast," said Uncle Ross, downing his champagne before having one of the handsome cater-waiters refill it. "To Corliss Meyers, my niece. She's made the last few months a total delight for so many of us. But now she has to go off to begin her fabulous future at Columbia University, where she will learn how to *help people in need*." He made the last part sound like he was throwing up in his mouth, but then he recovered to continue. "She's a class act, my niece. We're all going to miss her very much."

Corliss couldn't believe what she was hearing. *Sentiment? From Uncle Ross?*

Uncle Ross held his glass high. So did everyone else. They all looked even sadder now. Especially Max. Corliss felt a thickness in her throat and tried not to cry.

"To Corliss," they all said as they toasted.

"Can I just say something?" Corliss said. Everyone looked at her. "I don't want to get all mushy here, but you guys are the best. This isn't supposed to be a going-away party, though. It's the premiere of *The 'Bu!* The show we've all worked *so* hard to make good. Nothing can ever take that away from us. So let's toast *The 'Bu* again, okay? Uncle Ross, can I have a glass of real champagne for this?"

Uncle Ross's eyes opened so wide Corliss thought he'd hurt himself. "That's the spirit, Corliss—underage drinking! I knew Hollywood would open *all kinds of doors* for you."

As a handsome cater-waiter moved toward Corliss with a magnum of Dom Pérignon, everyone cheered. "To *The 'Bu!*" they all called out.

"To *The 'Bu*," came a familiar husky voice at the entrance to the VIP area. Everyone turned.

"Anushka," shouted Corliss. "You got the invite!" She then looked sheepishly at Max, who raised an eyebrow in her direction. "I'll explain later," Corliss mouthed to Max.

Anushka hit an imaginary mark on the floor, found the perfect light under one of the Chinese lanterns, and paused a beat while everyone gasped. She was resplendent in an electric-blue John Galliano minidress, six-inch Jimmy Choos, and a polka-dot lambskin clutch. "What's the matter? Haven't any of you ever seen a former TV star before?" She threw her head back and let out her signature "Ha!"

But there was nothing *former* about her. She still had it. And as she stepped into the roped-off VIP area, she made sure all of *it* was showing. She was teen perfection in motion. Her taut body, her gleaming skin, her luxurious buckwheat-colored hair—and those staggering lunar blue eyes. Everything was working for Anushka tonight.

She picked up a glass of champagne. "Come on, kids, let's forget old times and toast to new ones. That's why I'm here." She turned to Max. "Right, Max-y? Kiss, kiss. You know ya love me!" She winked and flirted and laughed—and it worked. Max blushed, recovered, and threw his arms around her. Everyone cheered and rushed to say hi to her. "Tans! Trent! Jeebster!" Anushka hugged them all and they all hugged her back.

"Anushka," yelped Tanya. "I so, so, so missed ya!"

"Anush, you little vixen," said JB, looking her up and down. "You look like all that and a bag of bling!"

"Yah," said Trent, "even though we're all, like, 'blech' around each other, I gotta admit you look so slammin' even I'd do you tonight."

"Thanks, lover," said Anushka, who proceeded to make a gagging sound.

"Anushka, I'm Corliss's Uncle Ross. I looooved you in *Suburban Magic*!"

"Nice to meetcha, Uncs. And now that it's a *real* party," she said to everyone, "what say we all hop in my limo outside and hit the town!"

"Come on, Uncle Ross," said Anushka. "Let's hit the Strip and take it up a notch! You too, Max."

"Well, it sounds like fun," said Max. "But tomorrow I promised Legend that I'd take him to Long Beach for 'Lisper's Little League.' Any child who lisps is given a bat and ball and made to feel utterly normal for one day. I have to get up very early and I can't let him down."

Anushka made a pouty face. "Well, we'll bring you in

spirit! What about the rest of you? Tomorrow's Thursday so there's no excuse!"

They all looked at each other like, "Is this going to be trouble?"

"What's the holdup?" said Anushka, hands on her hips, now her old bossy self again. "Okay, I'm paying!"

"Yay," shouted JB. "Color me there!" He ran out of the room.

"Sounds dope to me," said Trent.

"But what about my forty-seven cousins?" protested Tanya to Corliss. "They're out there somewhere in that area where the normal people are, and I haven't even said hello to them. Oh, I know what! I'll mail them all my autograph tomorrow so it doesn't look like I blew them off." She made her way out.

Corliss looked at Uncle Ross. "You coming?"

"No, thank you, darling. It's very sweet of you young people to keep in mind someone in his forties, but I'm going to go home and help Jurgen fold the chenille. One of our little Friday night routines. Now run along with your little friends and have fun, fun, fun." He kissed her on the forehead and headed out.

Corliss turned to Max. "That was a very nice greeting you gave to Anushka, Max."

"Keep your friends close, but keep your enemies closer."

"Wow. Who said that?"

"Me."

"But I mean before you?"

"I don't know, but whenever I quote something smart I

try and attribute it to myself."

"Well, Anushka is hardly your enemy, Max. I think you guys really *do* like each other deep down. Like *deep, deep* down. You sure you don't want to come along for at least a little bit? It's not that late. You could follow in your Porsche."

"Thanks, Corliss, but the truth is I'm exhausted. It's been a tough week. Even though the premiere went like gangbusters, I still haven't found Rocco and Michael Rothstein is breathing down my neck about it."

Corliss had been downwind of Michael Rothstein's breath a few times so she knew whereof Max spoke. "That can't be pleasant."

"No, indeed. If Rocco's not back to start filming the next episode, it's my head on a platter. And on top of *that*, even though I know you have been working overtime to uncover who is writing The 'Bu-hoo, we still don't know who it is."

Corliss nodded. "I know, Max. It's so frustrating, it's almost brought my eczema back!"

"TMI, Corliss."

"Sorry, but I've spent hours on the case and so far nothing, zilch, nada! Everyone either has an alibi or doesn't make sense as MBK. I'm stumped. And I really feel like I'm letting you down just as I'm about to go off forever. It's not how I want to leave things."

"Don't worry, Corliss. This is the toughest assignment you've had since you started working for *The 'Bu*. I know you're working hard."

"Thanks, Max." A horn honked on the street below. Corliss looked down. Anushka was next to her limo, waving wildly for Corliss to hurry it up. Corliss didn't want to leave

Max in his hour of need, but she *really* wanted to get in that limo. The limo honked again.

"You'd better go, Corliss."

"Really?"

"This could be your last night of fun in Los Angeles for some time. Put all this work stuff aside and enjoy yourself. You deserve it."

"Thanks, Max," she said, moving to go. "But you'd better get home and get some rest. Try and stop worrying about Rocco and The 'Bu-hoo for just one night. It might not be easy, but you have to come to grips with one fundamental psychological truth—that none of us has any control over anything!"

"Once again, Corliss, you carve me in two with your razor-sharp insight."

"That metaphor was a little wonky, Max, but I appreciate the sentiment. And who knows? Maybe I'll dig up some helpful information about MBK this evening."

"Corliss, seriously, just go and have fun like kids your age should. Leave the interrogating till tomorrow."

"Okay, Max, I promise." She kissed Max on the cheek and headed out.

Area—10:31 P.M.

Anushka and Corliss were dancing hard in the VIP area. Sweat poured from them, and their dresses clung tightly as they threw themselves around in circles.

"This is a total workout!" shouted Corliss over Britney Spears's recently leaked single.

"Nuthin' better than dancin'!" shouted Anushka back.

"Well, I can think of *one* thing better . . ."

Corliss swatted Anushka. *"You are so bad!"* Corliss looked around. In her dance frenzy, she'd lost track of the others. "Hey, where are the rest of us?"

"Trent and Tans are over there." Anushka nodded to the corner of the VIP section, where Trent and Tanya were dancing with other people while trying to make each other jealous. "And JB is there," she said, nodding to a tabletop nearby, where JB was writhing away like the go-go boy wannabe he wanted to be.

"Oh, dear," said Corliss on seeing JB, his glasses steamed up and his tuxedo shirt half out. "Maybe we should cut him off at the next Electric Lemonade."

"Naw, let the little guy have his fun. Besides, he's looking pretty zegxy tonight. I mean in that kind of pathetic, loser-y, hot way."

"Maybe to some people, but he'll always be nerdy, weird-y, slightly gay JB to me. Which is why I thought he might be writing The 'Bu-hoo. You'd have to be all those things to write that blog!"

"You think JB is MBK?!"

"I *did*, until I talked to him. I'm pretty convinced he's not, but I'm running out of suspects. I'd put my money on you, Anushka, except for the fact that you're kind of outside *The 'Bu* loop at the moment. You only know what I tell you about what goes on the set. And I make sure I don't tell you much!"

"You'd really put your money on *me* being MBK?! HA! That's a good one. But I've gotta tell you, Cor, I lap that thing up like a strawberry shake. And *mmmmm* is it good! I check it every day like clockwork just to read about Max falling on his face, day in and day out. Solid gold!"

A waitress came by wearing thigh-high white boots. She had the tiniest waist Corliss had ever seen and a look that defined *whatever*. Anushka signaled for her. "Two more Red Bulls and make it snappy, Attitude Girl!"

"Don't you want a real drink?" the tiny-waisted waitress droned. "Your table does have bottle service."

Anushka's eyes narrowed. "Just the Red Bull, *danke*."

The waitress gave Anushka a *whatever* look and peeled off. Corliss was impressed. "Wow, Anushka. Red Bull without a vodka chaser? Are you off the poison?"

"Booze-free for twenty-one days now! Even though I've had seventeen Red Bulls today. Cor, child, I am so high on caffeine my nipples hurt."

Corliss laughed. "Well at least you're not facedown on my Steve Maddens like you were the last time we hung out."

"It's a whole new Anushka! Studying hard, stone-cold sober, and looking fierce!" She did a spectacular hip swivel to punctuate the last part. "The truth is," she said, moving close to Corliss so she could whisper, "I'm gearing up to get my spectacular bod back on *The 'Bu*."

"*What?*" shrieked Corliss, who then tried to match Anushka's hip swivel but hurt herself in the process.

"Calm down, kiddo. It's only in the planning stages at the moment. But I've fired all my agents and managers and hired a whole buncha new ones. We're hatching this master plan to completely show the world how I've *totally* rehabilitated myself by going to school and being a good girl—gag—and how I'm completely sorry for every unprofessional thing I've ever done—barf—and how such a *huge* talent as mine shouldn't go to waste studying psychology—no offense. But blah, blah, you get the picture. If I build back up my fan base and create enough noise, I could be back on *The 'Bu* by the end of this season."

Corliss was impressed. There was only one problem with Anushka's plan. "Anushka, your character *died* in the pilot."

Anushka rolled her eyes. "Details, details. That's what writers are for. Trust me, Cor, things are looking up for *moi*. The only thing missing is a boyfriend. Which I plan on finding tonight! I'll find one for you, too, if you're lucky." Anushka scanned the room for eligible boy booty.

"Wow, Anushka, I sure hope your plan works. I think *The 'Bu* misses you! As for the boyfriend search, it's *so* not my focus at the moment. Besides, I'm heading off to New York in three days. If there was any chance of hell freezing over and me meeting a boy tonight, what would I do with him? Put him in my luggage and show up with him at my Evolving Stigma of Bipolarity class next week?"

"Why not? Shake that school up a little. Or leave him on a baggage carousel at LAX! What do I care? You think *way* too much about the future, Cor. Let's find you a hottie boyfriend and concentrate on *tonight*."

"Anushka, I can't have a relationship for *three days*."

"Cor, some of my *best* relationships have been for three days! You don't have to hang out with their friends, be introduced to their mother, or in some cases even learn their names. Now let's take a walk into this zegxy, zegxy crowd to find ourselves some prime beef!" Anushka took Corliss's hand and yanked her into the sweaty throng.

"Okay, Anushka, but it can't be a late evening. I've got to start packing tomorrow!"

Anushka's Penthouse—1:37 A.M.

The place was packed with bodies and the music was cranked. Way cranked. Kanye West was thump-thump-thumpin'. Beautiful people danced, bounced, shouted, and grinded. They were on the balcony, they were on the floor, they were draped across the sofas, they were climbing on the piano. Glam Hollywood teen pandemonium.

Corliss checked her watch. *Sweet Louise, I have to get up and starting packing for my trip! How am I ever gonna find Anushka in this mess?* Last she knew, fifty or so scenesters were literally picking Anushka up over their heads and carting her off somewhere. Corliss hoped her friend wasn't off in some corner up to no good.

"Hey, Cor, do you think Anushka is off in some corner up to no good?" It was JB, tugging at her from out of nowhere. He looked like a wreck. His tuxedo shirt was torn to shreds and his glasses were missing a lens.

"JB, my God! What happened to you?"

"I'm not sure," he said. "After about the third Electric Lemonade I started losing things."

"Are you okay?" Corliss had never seen him like this.

"I'm great! I think it's high-time the Jeebster cut loose, don't you?"

"Go crazy, JB. You deserve it. Especially after the grilling I gave you the other day. I was just doing my job. You know that, right? I know you can't be MBK. I'm really sorry, and

I'll find a way to make it up to you somehow." JB waved this off. He actually looked really cute all messed up and smiling crookedly at Corliss. "Can you believe this place? I'm surprised the hotel doesn't throw Anushka out on her over-publicized tush."

"Are you kidding? The Sunset Tower *lives* for this kind of publicity. You know who's in this penthouse?" Corliss shook her head. "Ashton Kutcher is playing poker in the kitchen, Keira Knightley is over by the fireplace, and Scarlett Johansson is right over there by the freestanding ashtrays!"

JB stood up and started to teeter off in the direction of Scarlett Johansson. Corliss stopped him. "Whoa, cowboy. You sure you can make it all the way across the room without falling off your horse?"

JB opened his mouth to answer, weaved a little bit, then fell backward on two bellboys who'd fallen asleep spooning.

"JB, you're sitting on two bellboys."

He looked down. "That is the second time that's happened tonight!" He moved to the floor, resting his head against the back of a sofa. Corliss sat next to him. As the party swirled above them, Corliss felt safe in their sort-of hiding place. But she could tell something was wrong with JB.

"What is it?"

"I know I should be happy, but I feel like such a screwup."

Corliss knew what was wrong. "JB, no one blames you for those little, um, online escapades."

"They don't?"

"Well, some people do—but I don't. Addiction is a psychological condition. Look at Trent and Rocco! Addiction makes people do and say and behave in all kinds of ways they wouldn't normally want to."

Just then someone dumped a vodka cranberry on JB's head.

"Case in point," Corliss said, stifling the urge to giggle.

"What do I look like," asked JB, "some kind of slop sink?"

"Look," said Corliss, scrounging up some tissues from her purse so she could wipe JB's face, "I'm here for you, JB. I owe a lot to you. You're responsible for the Corliss Meyers Beverly Hills makeover. I've gone from dowdy to fairly style-y because of you."

"Aw, shucks."

"I'm not kidding! I'm here for all my 'Bu friends. I just wish I could out who's writing the blog already. But in the meantime, I just wish everyone would stop reading it!"

"But, Cor, The 'Bu-hoo is addictive, too! Every morning I get up, reach for the Fruit Loops, and sign on to get the new dirt. It's not the best part of the Jeebster, but I can't help it."

"Apparently, you're not the only one," said Corliss, casting yet another glance around the room for Anushka.

"Don't be disappointed in me, Corliss. I'm just a skinny little dude from Tarzana without a life of his own. I can't help it if I want to live through other people—even people I'm working with!"

"Vicarious living never got anyone anywhere, JB. That's Psychology 101."

The fact was, Corliss really *was* disappointed in JB. Not because of his slightly sketchy recent past, but because he was no longer paying attention to her. Scarlett Johansson was bending over in front of them, straightening out her black tights, and the sight seemed to transfix her geeky little friend. "Oh, forget it, you'd obviously rather stare up you-know-who-over-there's skirt."

"Guilty as charged!" he shouted, scaring Scarlett Johansson away.

Corliss stood up, brushed herself off, and waved bye-bye to JB, wedging herself into the slippery crowd and heading toward what she hoped was the door. En route she found Anushka bouncing on 50 Cent's lap. Ten feet later she stumbled across Tanya and Trent making out wildly in line for the bathroom. *I guess that was bound to happen sooner or later.* And in the foyer, just as she cleared the worst of the throng, her eyes fell upon Jack Black doing a Daniel Radcliffe imitation. "Boy," she said to herself, "if that isn't a reason to say good night I don't know what is."

Somewhere, Sometime—Early the Next Morning

'*Bu*-lovers, the news is '*Bu*-rageous! '*Bu*-abulous! '*Bu*-pendous! It's finally happened! The show aired! *The 'Bu* flew!

For those of you living under a gigantic rock, *The 'Bu* pilot premiered on the struggling UBC network last night. And Hannah Montana on a popsicle stick was it good!

The fiery climax! Anushka's untimely demise! The bodacious tatas! Now y'all know what I've been hopped up about this whole time. *HOLLA.*

And just as Goth Roth predicted, the overnight ratings are through the freakin' roof!! The UBC is now back on tippity-top, Goth Roth just got a promotion to Largest Man Ever to Squeeze Into Lycra, and M2 can finally pay off that crazy see-through house in the hills!!! Time to renegotiate your contracts, people. ; - p

The success of *The 'Bu* means, of course, two other things. And they are *muy, muy importante.*

Rocco better get his Versace-wearin' butt back from Sicily faster than you can say spaghettini.

(And this is the most *muy importante.*) The *'Bu*-hoo—and MBK (yours *'Bu*-ly)—will now become an even more important player in the daily *'Bu* drama.

Dats right. Give it up for MBK, peeps. I've got me more power ;)p Dontcha think I deserve it??? HA! I do.

And to think M2 thought he could bring me down! NEVER! He really thought he could dispatch Columbia-bound Clueless Meyers to uncover my identity???? Poor thing is looking high and low, meanwhile, I'm right under her cheese-sniffing, Indiana-no-place nose!

In fact, Clueless is soooo out of it she's also TOTALLY unaware that M2 is packing his own devastating secret. One that MBK has uncovered! That's right, folks. Mr. Judgemento himself has a secret so epic and juicy it's sure to put everyone else's pissy-caca secrets to shame. Ya hear me? TO SHAME!

BUT! I can only give you ONE hint about M2's secret right now. The rest will hafta wait till later! You ready to be teased about M2's secret????

It involves someone not as tall as he is.

Huh? What? Come again please?!?

That's all I'm sayin' for now, suckas!

But as a consolation prize for checking in, I've got some real dirty dirt I CAN tell you all about. It concerns Petey Newsome, M2's head writer, Anushka Peter's one-time booze buddy, and chronic crusher of Clueless Meyers. So step up, Petey, yours is the next head on MBK's chopping block.

Why, you ask? I'll tells ya!

Seems little Petey hasn't been so honest with the Human Resources department of the UBC network. His paperwork says that he graduated Harvard this year. That makes him twenty-one or twenty-two, right? Nope, our friend Petey is not twenty-two, or twenty-one, or even twenty! Check it: The dude is seventeen. Petey never even made it to college! Forget Harvard, little

Petey Newsome barely made it out of Cherry Hill Senior High.

Talk about DRAMA.
Seems that kid was mad cruisin' for some good old-fashioned Hollywood success—success that he'd stop at nothing to get! So he invented an entire larger-than-life, brilliant background for himself.

Paging Dr. Phil!

. . . complete with made-up résumé . . .

SEE KEYWORDS: forged college diploma

. . . and bought a one-way ticket to the UBC offices.

CLICK HERE FOR: <u>Department of Labor Unemployment Division</u>

What can I tell ya? Petey Newsome just ain't who he says he is. How effed up is THAT?

Gee, I hope I haven't put the poor kid in a bad position . . . But MBK knows all, my kiddies! And it sometimes *pains* me, this burden. Having the power to reveal and destroy . . . but I've got to! I've got to rid the world of hypocrisy! That is my mission!

So stay tuned, *'Bu*-busters. 'Cause the bigger *The 'Bu* gets, the more I'm gonna *rock your world*.

Yours in *'Bu*-nificent *'Bu*-dom,
MBK

Eight

Petey stood before Max's desk, quivering. "I can explain everything, Max."

But Max didn't want to hear it. He'd been up all night on the phone with the Sicilian Coast Guard trying to determine if Rocco had boarded George Clooney's seaplane or not. Max raised a hand to Petey, giving him his patented "please cease" gesture.

"That's y-y-your 'please, cease' gesture," stammered Petey. "Don't I get to defend myself?"

Max always knew there was something about Petey he didn't like. Now he had his proof. "Petey, I don't make drastic decisions lightly. Now, I'm sure you have your reasons for misrepresenting yourself to us as a brilliant young writer, but the fact is, after a few phone calls this morning, I find out what you are is a not-so-brilliant, way-too-young imposter."

"But, Max, the pilot was a hit—the pilot I wrote! The

UBC network is back on top because of it. You and everyone involved in *The 'Bu* are going to become rich because of *the pilot I wrote.* H-h-how can you say I'm not what I say I am?"

Max knew Petey had a point. He looked at his cuticles for a moment in order to buy time while he considered his response. He noticed they looked especially healthy this morning and made a note in his iPhone that the zinc pills he was now taking seemed to be doing the trick. *My cuticles are so shiny and healthy and perfectly shaped—*

"Max, how can you be admiring your cuticles when my career is on the line?!" Petey hollered like a madman.

Max sighed and looked at his watch. There wasn't time for letting Petey down easy. "Here's the thing, Petey. You may have 'written' the pilot as you say, but it was my impromptu brilliance during the filming of the pilot that put it over the edge. *I* was the one who incorporated real footage of the Malibu Canyon fire into the pilot, creating a stunning blend of imagery that seared into the minds of the American audience. It was a brilliant gesture on my part and had nothing to do with any writer's mere *words*."

"But—"

"Besides, it doesn't matter because, although I tried to fire you repeatedly, your contract up until this point kept me from doing so. Now that you're not the age you said you were, which means you have no legal working papers, your contract is null and void."

"Null? Void?"

"Yes," said Max, admiring his cuticles once more.

"Null and void, both. You can talk to Legal if you have any questions. There will, of course, be no severance paycheck, buyout, or other compensation. Basically you're out on your teenage bum."

"But—but—what will I do? Where will I go?"

"Don't be so dramatic, Petey. You're seventeen. You can probably work the grill at In-N-Out Burger."

"Oh my God," said Petey, looking faint.

Max pressed the intercom on this desk phone. "Corliss, can you come in, please? I'll need my mid-early morning snack of organic lemonade sweetened with Agave nectar and six flame-roasted chestnuts. If there are any wasabi peas out there you can bring in three, *but no more*. You should also bring in some aspirin and a latte for Petey, whom I've just fired."

Petey sunk down into the leather sofa opposite Max's desk and put his hand to his head. "It's over . . . all I see is black."

"That's because that's all you ever wear. You might try to incorporate a little color every now and then."

Corliss bounded through the door with a tray on which sat Max's snacks and a latte and aspirin for Petey. "What happened?" she asked as she gave Petey the aspirin and latte. "You got fired? But I thought your contract—?"

"Null! Void!"

Max gave Corliss a level look. "It had to happen, Corliss."

"But Max, Petey was the last writer standing! You fired all the others, remember?"

"And how does this ultimately concern me, Corliss?"

Corliss slammed down the tray. Max's mid-early morning snacks rattled.

"Corliss, that made a noise."

"Boy, Max, I was hoping my last week on the job would be a little more peaceful. But you never fail to amaze!"

"Corliss, your tone is brittle and unappealing."

"I think she sounds kind of sweet," said Petey, smiling bashfully at Corliss.

"You," she said, turning to Petey, "cool it. You just got canned. Time to stop flirting and start strategizing." She turned to Max. "And *you* have got to come up with a script that explains why Rocco's character is not around. In two days! With no writers!"

Max felt his stomach tie itself into a complicated knot. "My God, Corliss . . . you're right."

"Of course I'm right!"

Petey raised his hand. "My job back, please?"

Max knew it wasn't as easy as that. "Your contract is null and void!"

"Null!" Petey wailed. "Void!"

"What are we going to do?" wailed Max. "I've been up all night with the Sicilian Coast Guard and I'm sleep deprived! And Michael Rothstein called me from his Yogalates class today and cursed at me, which made me feel tiny and insignificant! To top it off, I have to suffer the indignity of reading in The 'Buhoo that I have some awful secret—which I *don't*. Scientology pounds every awful secret out of you until you're 'clear'! Which means see-through, or something. I keep forgetting to read that book!"

"Null and void!" bellowed Petey.

"Stop shouting, everyone!" said Corliss. "Especially you, Max, because of your upper girly register thing. Put The 'Bu-hoo aside for one moment. We have to think about this writer situation—and fast. I'm on a plane to New York in a couple days. You'll have to handle all of this *on your own* when I'm gone. I won't be around to offer you brilliantly shrewd suggestions, or whatever you said they were."

"You won't . . ." said Max, who looked at Corliss, his competent wonder, his best assistant ever, and suddenly felt lighter than air.

"What is it, Max? You're smiling like a crazy person."

"Corliss, it's *you*."

"What's me?"

"This is brilliant! It's always you!" Max laughed and clapped.

"You're scaring me, Max."

"Yeah," said Petey, who looked jealous. "What exactly do you mean?"

"What I mean is that *you*, Corliss, should do the rewrite on the second episode!" Max felt this was such a magnificent idea that he decided to punctuate it by sitting back in his chair and putting his feet up. His shoes immediately distracted him. *These Testoni loafers are so luxurious, he thought. I wonder if Barneys has them in black?*

"Max," said Corliss, who looked stunned. "I think you're hitting that Agave way too hard. First of all, didn't you want me to spend every waking hour before I left trying to crack The 'Bu-hoo mystery? And second, and most important, I can't write!"

"She *can't* write!" said Petey.

"Hey," said Corliss. "How do *you* know?"

"Because you just said it," said Petey, pouting.

Max knew he had to stop admiring his footwear if he was going to make his point. "Corliss, to answer your questions, solving the mystery of who MBK is won't be necessary if there isn't a *'Bu* for MBK to blog about, right? And second, you obviously *can* write. Your reports are flawless. I have reams and reams of your writing since the first day you got here."

"But," said Corliss, "that kind of writing has nothing to do with the kind of writing a television script requires!"

"Exactly! It's not the same!" shouted Petey petulantly.

"Petey," said Corliss, exasperated. "Do you think you can leave Max and me alone for a moment?"

"Yes," said Max. "You should probably be putting in an application at In-N-Out Burger by now."

"Okay," said Petey, standing, looking hurt, "but this isn't the last you're going to hear from Petey Newsome!" He left the trailer and slammed the door so hard a framed photo of Max and Claire Danes smashed to the floor. Corliss immediately went to clean it up.

"Don't worry about that, Corliss. You have a script to write."

"But I've never written a script before!" said Corliss, shrieking.

"Now who sounds girly in their upper register?"

"But I am a girl!" Corliss shrieked even louder. "One who has *never written a script before!*"

"Corliss, sit down and take a giant chill pill. You have a subtle grasp of people's psychological motivations. That's all you need. Besides, JB mentioned to me that you had some good ideas for this season."

"He did?"

"Yes, he said you and he were hanging out with Anushka, and you told the both of them some great ideas."

Corliss had absolutely no recollection of ever saying such a thing. But she couldn't recall much at this moment. Everything seemed to be going dark, and the walls seemed to be tilting toward her, creating a tomb-like space in which breathing was becoming very, very difficult. "Max, okay, please, I'm sitting down, I'm calming down, and this is an amazing offer and everything, don't get me wrong. I'm just a near-sighted girl from Indianapolis with a few humble dreams and a new wardrobe. But here's the thing, and it's a big one—the timing sucks!"

"It sucks?"

"Yes! I'm supposed to fly to New York in a couple days to go to school next Monday."

"So, that gives us two days, Corliss," Max said as if it were the most reasonable thing in the world. "I say take the afternoon off and start writing. We'll see what you've got at the end of two days and take it from there."

"But what if all I've come up with at the end of two days is an incoherent mess of bad writing?"

"Corliss," said Max, leaning over the table and looking at her with his piercing gray eyes. "What other choice do I have?"

Anushka's Penthouse—2:12 P.M.

"Open up, Anushka. I know you're in there!" There was no answer. "Come on, I really need you!"

Finally, the door creaked open. Anushka peeked out. "Do I know you?"

"Quit the hijinks and let me in."

Anushka opened the door and Corliss skittered inside. She couldn't believe the mess. "You haven't cleaned since the party?"

"Oh, yeah, sorry. I just hate the cleaning lady they send up. She looks at me, like, *who do you think you are to be making such a mess?* And then I look at her, like, *who do you think you are to look at me like who do you think you are?*"

"Sounds like a vicious cycle."

"Totally."

"Listen, Anushka, I'd love to stay and chat with you about how hard it is to be young and famous and rich with a cleaning lady who resents you because of it, but I'm in BIG trouble."

"Oh, no!" Anushka called out, clutching her heart dramatically. "I thought for sure you knew how to use birth control!"

"No, for God's sake, not that! And it would totally have to be an immaculate conception, if you know what I mean."

"Then what's wrong, Cor? Sit down. I've got a pitcher of Arnold Palmers in the fridge. JB taught me how to make them at the party. Of course a shot of Ketel One wouldn't hurt, but as you know I am totally on the wagon. And I suggest you stay sober yourself. You look like a woman on the verge of a nervous wipe-out. Be back in a minute."

"Thanks, Anushka. You're the best." Corliss sat and collected herself. The tables had really turned . . . Anushka was being the calm, cool, and collected one while Corliss was suddenly the troubled teen.

"Here you go," said Anushka, coming back into the room with a nice, tall Arnold Palmer. "Now take a sip, chase it with a deep breath, and gimme the 411."

"Thanks," said Corliss, sipping and breathing. "Phew! I called JB to come over, too—he's also responsible for this mess."

"You're sure you're not pregnant?"

Corliss swatted Anushka. "Stop saying that! And JB and I are totally and only friends. Even if he *did* look really cute last night."

Anushka wiggled her eyebrows. "Uh-huh."

"Stop it! Listen, the thing is Max finally fired Petey because this morning on The 'Bu-hoo it said Petey is not a twenty-two-year-old prodigy from Harvard but a seventeen-year-old nobody from Cherry Hill!"

"*What?* That little fake! And I took him down to Tijuana to buy *beer* because I didn't want to pass a fake ID! You mean to tell me *he* was passing a fake ID, and we *could have* ended up in a Mexican jail?"

"Apparently. Fake ID, fake résumé, fake everything! The truth is that Petey is really suffering from a psychological condition which, if I had a degree, I would diagnose to be a result of impaired development dueto—"

"Skip the lecture, prof, I get enough of it at school."

"Sorry. So anyway, now that Petey's revealed to be

an underage nobody from Cherry Hill, his contract with the network is null and void. And since Max fired all the other writers, this means there are *no writers left*. Not a one! So— brace yourself, America—Max asked ME to write the second episode. ME!"

Anushka inhaled so hard she toppled off the ottoman she'd been perched on. Corliss helped her up. "And not only does it have to be a good episode, it has to explain why Rocco's character, Ramone, is all of a sudden nowhere to be found! Because Rocco himself is still nowhere to be found."

"Cor, I don't know what to say. This is *big*. This is huge! Of course, all I can do is think about myself at a moment like this. Because if you do a really good job with this episode, by the time I weasel my way back onto *The 'Bu*, you could be writing episodes all about me!" There was an insistent knocking at the door. "Go away, judge-y cleaning person!" said Anushka.

"But it's me," came JB's voice. "The Jeebster, defender of all that is good and honorable in the world! Especially if it's wearing a minidress!"

Anushka rolled her eyes and leaped to answer the door. "If I let you in, are you going to be a total dork?"

"Partial, perhaps," came the reply.

"Let him in, Anushka, this is a time-sensitive conversation! I'm supposed to go to New York and begin school this coming Monday. I don't know how I can write an episode in two days—or ever!"

"Cool your jets, Cor. I bet JB will have an idea." Anushka let JB in. He rushed over to Corliss with a look of panic.

"What is it, Corliss? On your message you sounded as nervous as a bag of cats."

"Thanks, JB. In fact, I'm *more* nervous than a bag of cats. I'm more like a bag of monkeys with fleas. In fact, I'm totally configured in a torturous mind-warp of gigundo proportions."

"Wow," said JB, "expressive."

"Thanks," said Corliss. "I'm trying to get my writer on."

"Huh?" said JB.

"Here's the thing," said Anushka, taking over. "Max fired Petey 'cause he's a seventeen-year-old loser, not a twenty-two-year-old genius. There are no writers left on staff 'cause Petey was the last pasty-face standing. Max wants Cor to write the second episode, which has to explain why Rocco's character, Ramone, is missing in action. We all know Rocs is actually drying out his 'roids at some schmancy island resort, but the audience has to think Ramone's absence is a *'Bu* plot twist. Oh, and Corliss has to figure it all out in two days. Get it?"

JB inhaled so hard his asthma kicked in. He took out his inhaler and calmed himself down.

"I know," said Corliss. "Pretty hard to swallow, right? And *the two of you* are to blame because apparently you told Max I had great ideas for shows!"

"I didn't tell Max nuttin'," said Anushka, shaking her head. "We had one kissy-face moment at the party at Grauman's, which I only put up with because I'm angling to get my zegxy zelf back on *The 'Bu*."

"You are?" said JB, as his asthma kicked in again.

"You didn't hear it from me, Jeebs." She mimed

zipping her mouth shut. "I swear, Cor, I haven't said two words to that pretentious fakity-fake Max Marx since I set Malibu Canyon on fire and he canned my gorgeous butt. Certainly not about your writing abilities. Wait, do you *have* any?"

"No?!" Corliss turned to JB. "Then it was *you* who said something to Max?"

JB looked guilty. "I'm afraid I think I might maybe have said something to Max about you maybe having some sort of ideas for *'Bu* stories . . ."

"Great, thanks a lot! Now I've got two days to try and come up with a script before I fly to New York. Which wouldn't be so hellacious if I had any talent—or ideas. Which I don't! Neither talent nor ideas!"

The phone rang. Anushka picked it up. "AP here, speak when spoken to! What? Oh, hi, Dimitri, so sorry. What? OHMYGOD! I'll be right there." She slammed the phone down and flew like the wind into her shoe closet.

"What is it, Anushka?" said Corliss.

Anushka could be heard tossing shoes from the shelves. "OHMYGOD, Dimitri, the concierge, just called up to say Orlando Bloom is headed for the pool. He's by himself and looks totally dreamy! Can you believe it?!"

Corliss's heart sank. *How can she think about boy booty at a time like this? Doesn't she know I'm having a crisis?*

"Anushka," pleaded JB. "Corliss is in trouble. Can't you put aside your free-range libido for one afternoon?"

"Sorry kids," said Anushka, appearing back in the room in a dangerously tiny Betsey Johnson bikini and six-inch

Vivienne Westwood heels. "When it comes to Orlando and his Bloom, I am a heat-seeking missile."

"Wow," said JB. "Sure you don't want to stay here and show us every angle?"

Anushka twirled around so they could see every angle. JB applauded.

"Let her go, JB," said Corliss. "Nothing gets between Anushka and her quest for Bloom."

With that, Anushka beat a path out the door, and Corliss let out a giant sigh. "What am I going to do, JB?" She moved closer to him and instinctively put her head on his shoulder. Then she wondered why she had done that. She decided to keep it there, because taking it away might seem awkward. But then she wondered if keeping it there would make JB think she was coming on to him. She was so torn up. Her change of duties from MBK seeker to 'Bu writer had left her mind reeling.

After a moment, JB put his hand on her knee. Corliss's wondering began all over again. Was JB putting his hand on her knee in a sexy way? Or in an I-feel-bad-for-pathetic-Corliss way? Was her comrade-in-geek-arms sending her a not-so-subtle signal that he'd like to take their relationship to the love level? And when would her wondering stop?

"You'll be great, Cor. You can write it! You're way talented at so many things. And you *did* have good ideas about shows. You were full of ideas that night you, me, and Anushka went to Matsuhisa, and I put wasabi up my nose. Don't you remember?"

"I was full of crab maki! And, no, I don't remember having any ideas." She knew she had to steady herself. She was heading fast to Overstimulation Land. "JB?"

"Yeah?"

"Your hand is kinda, like, on my knee. Which means it's in close proximity to my thigh."

"It is?" He looked. "Sweet Carrie Underwood, how did that happen?!" He withdrew his hand.

"You know what?" said JB, suddenly standing. "I gotta go. Vamoose, hit the road, skedaddle."

"What?! Just like that?"

"Yeah, I forgot there's a *Buffy the Vampire Slayer* fan club meeting tonight at this church basement in the Valley."

"I've never heard you mention that you liked that show before."

"I haven't? Well, I do! I love it! All those girl vampires doing, you know, sexy girl vampire things! Can't get enough!" he said, dashing from Anushka's penthouse. He ran so fast he forgot to close the door behind him. Corliss ran after him to stop him at the elevator, but he was beating a path down the stairs—fourteen flights down.

"Great," said Corliss, returning alone to the penthouse. "Abandoned for some cult show that's not even on TV anymore *and* robbed of the vague promise of boy booty. Do I not rate or what?"

Nine

Uncle Ross's House—the Breakfast Room—7:18 A.M.

"Uncle Ross—"

"Please, Corliss," said Uncle Ross at the head of the breakfast table, "indoor voice. Uncle Ross had quite a late evening last night."

"The Ice Capades were in town again?"

"Very witty, Corliss. But no. Jurgen and I were up till all hours playing Posh and Becks. It's become a kind of ritual with us. And, well, we broke some furniture using it as the goalpost, and now poor Jurgen is upstairs taking a good steam because his glutes are sore."

"I'm not sure I know what you mean, although I am sure I totally don't want you to explain it. I guess what you're telling me is you're hungover?"

"Precisely. That's why I'm wearing this ice eye-mask and speaking in hushed tones."

"Okay," said Corliss, lowering her voice. "But I need help. I was up all night trying to think of what to write for the second episode and came up with nada!"

"Corliss, you know I don't speak Mexican."

"Nothing is what I came up with! I get on a plane tomorrow, and Max is expecting some sort of draft from me. I have to call him and tell him I just can't do it. I have to put an end to this madness and just say, 'Max, thank you, but you've got the wrong girl. You have to hire a proper writer. I'm clueless!' Which is what they call me on The 'Bu-hoo, by the way. Can you believe it?"

"I know, I got a good giggle out of that. Clueless Meyers! You've got to admit it's clever."

"Uncle Ross, I'm your niece!"

Uncle Ross took his ice eye-mask off and dropped it in his Bloody Mary. "Corliss, don't you see what's happening?"

"You've put your ice mask in your drink again?"

"Oh, dear, force of habit. No, I wasn't referring to that. I'm referring to the fabulous opportunity in front of you. Don't you know how many clueless, near-sighted girls from Indiana would give their eye teeth to write an episode of a new hit show?"

"What are eye teeth?"

"Corliss, keep up with me. You will not call Max back and tell him you can't do this. You will make a different call."

"I will?"

"Yes, a call to the good folks at Columbia University." Uncle Ross squinted toward the kitchen. "Where is the chef with my egg-white tartine?"

"Wait, wait—off topic with the tartine! Why should I call Columbia and not Max?"

"Because, my dear girl, you will tell them that you need

to defer your enrollment for a semester."

Corliss thought her head would pop off. "What?!"

"Everyone defers school for a semester here or there. You have an extremely important job at the moment. A job that could change the course of what's been a rather unremarkable life up to this moment. It's way too *tres* important for you to leave Los Angeles now. You must stay with *The 'Bu* and see it through. It's destiny calling, Corliss, can't you hear it?"

"No! I only hear the staff cursing at you in the kitchen. Uncle Ross, I'm so confused. I'm halfway out the door! All my *High School Musical* DVDs are already packed."

Uncle Ross sighed heavily. "When oh when is Zac Efron going to have his own musical?"

Just then, Uncle Ross's chef came in and slammed down the long-coming egg-white tartine. Uncle Ross winced. "High time. Were you waiting for the hens to lay the eggs?" The chef snorted and stomped off to the kitchen. Uncle Ross snorted back. "The attitude of a metropolitan star!"

"Uncle Ross, please—focus. I don't think I have the talent to write! You can't ask me to give up college for something I'm not sure I can even do."

"But Corliss, I'm not saying give up. I'm saying put off. For one measly semester. I know it sounds scary, and not at all according to plan, but trust me: It will probably work out. You must have the writing gene. It runs in our family. And, frankly, Corliss, I don't mean to be tough on you, but sometimes you have to throw yourself into the sky and build your wings on the way down."

"Wow," thought Corliss, transported by the thought. "Did you make that up?"

"Make what up?" said Uncle Ross, distracted once again and clicking his spoon against his empty Bloody Mary. "The thing is, college will always be there. Hollywood comes a-knocking only a very few times. It's your life, Corliss. I just want to make sure it's not full of regrets."

This went right through Corliss. She'd known so many people back in Indiana-no-place with regrets. People who'd missed their chances in life and were now working at Cracker Barrel in the mall, handing out samples of cheddar cheese on melba toast. Did she want to become one of them?

But then again, hadn't she worked so hard all through high school to make herself a viable candidate for an Ivy League education? One that would prepare her to help emotionally disturbed people not just on TV shows but wherever they happened to be?

Still, maybe Uncle Ross was right . . . school could wait. It was only one semester and, after all, Hollywood did seem to be calling. She thought about how fast things could change in such a short time. She'd gone from Max Marx's assistant to staff writer in less than a year. Maybe it was just the beginning of a climb to the very top of the Hollywood heap.

Corliss's heart raced exactly like it did whenever she had one of her premonitions. Something she couldn't explain was pushing her toward taking Uncle Ross's advice—which is something she almost never did.

"Okay, Uncle Ross. You know what? I'll do it."

"Do what?" said Uncle Ross, confused yet again.

"Hello?! Call Columbia and tell them I'm deferring admission for a semester."

"Oh, yes, that! Sorry, I've been contemplating Zac

Efron's floppy hair ever since we stopped talking a few moments back. Well, good job, Corliss! Try your hand at being a writer. I will support you with every ounce of my being. Now get upstairs to your room and start typing. This could be the first day of the rest of your . . . something."

"My life?"

Uncle Ross looked stumped. "I think it had something to do with Zac Efron but it's gone now . . ."

"Whatever, Uncle Ross. My mind is made up!" Corliss stood from the table triumphantly. "I'm going upstairs to write!"

"Corliss, wait!"

"What is it, Uncle Ross?"

"Something just occurred to me. And I don't mean to take the wind out of your sails, but don't you think you should call your mother and ask her permission? She is paying your college tuition after all."

"Yikes," said Corliss, her heart sinking as fast as it had risen. "That is a little bit of a hiccup in the plan." She laughed weakly. "I don't suppose you'd call her for me, Uncle Ross?"

Uncle Ross grinned. "Good as done, m'lady. Now run upstairs and start writing. I have a feeling once I explain everything to her the answer will be yes!"

"You're the best, Uncle Ross," said Corliss as she ran upstairs, taking two steps at a time.

Corliss's Room—Four Hours Later

Corliss was splayed across her desk in despair. She looked at her computer monitor for what must have been the thousandth time . . . but there was nothing. A black screen. No words. Nada.

A soft rapping came at the door. "Go away, Uncle Ross. It's not pretty in here."

"I just wanted you to know I finally got your mother on the phone about deferring school for a semester," said Uncle Ross from the hall outside her door. "After the screaming stopped, I really think she understood. Of course, she said she'd blame me if your future ends up in the toilet. I assured her it wouldn't be the first time I'd taken such blame. So you're good to go! Doesn't that make you happy?"

Corliss groaned.

"Are you having trouble in there? Let me in, Corliss. I'm sure I have just the thing that will help you work."

Corliss sighed, unstuck herself from the saliva that bound her to an empty legal pad, and trudged over to the door, which she unlocked. Uncle Ross stood in the hall with a tray of martinis.

"What's that?"

"Hendrick's, up with olives, what does it look like?"

"Uncle Ross, it's not even noon."

"Corliss, I know you're having trouble. I can hear you banging your head against the wall through the vents."

"Oh, sorry," she said, rubbing her forehead. "I think I have a scab."

"And, as an award-winning writer myself, I have a few tricks up my sleeve to help me start writing."

Corliss couldn't believe him. "What, getting hammered while the sun is still up?"

"Well, yes, to put it rather indelicately."

"Uncle Ross, we've been through this a million times. I am underage. I'm not allowed to drink. Does the word underage have any meaning for you?"

"Underage, smunderage," he said, bringing the tray of martinis into Corliss's room. "Corliss, you think 'drinking' refers to the cheap-flavored liquor and wine cooler-y things your mother drinks. Smirnoff Ice, for God's sake! Booze you can buy at the 7-Eleven. This is Hendrick's Gin, completely top shelf."

Corliss sighed and looked at her watch.

"And I am only trying to help. Many, many successful writers are alcoholics, and I just want you to look at it as an option. Of course, many successful writers who drink die terrible deaths in car crashes, boating accidents, et cetera, but they are always glamorous deaths—and that's the point."

Corliss thought she might scream. "Uncle Ross, you are not helping! You are being a total enabler, which is a psychological term for someone who's constantly trying to get someone else to drink!"

"Huh," he said, thoughtfully. "I didn't know there was a psychological term for what I am."

"There is—enabler!" She knew, however, that his intentions were good. "Look, I'm sorry to be all shout-y. It's just that I can't believe I set this whole thing in motion. Now that Mom's signed off on it, there's no turning back. I have to call Columbia and make the deferment a reality! And then somehow I have to deliver a script—while my brain feels like it's in a straitjacket."

"Writer's block," said Uncle Ross, nodding an understanding nod.

"Exactly! I think I should just be alone and try to figure this out. I'm sorry."

Uncle Ross looked hurt. "All right, Corliss. But I'll leave the martinis just in case. You might get curious, you never know." With that, Uncle Ross withdrew.

Corliss paced around the room wondering what would get her head unlocked. *Now I know why writers hit the sauce—it's a hard job! You have to be alone! And think things up! And then type the things you're thinking up! Argggg!*

Corliss sat herself back at her desk again. But it was hopeless. The tray of martinis sat glistening a few feet from her head. She kept catching sight of the silver martini shaker out of the corner of her eye. It had glistening beads of water on it. The tall martini glass next to it was made of Waterford crystal. The bottle of Hendrick's, with its distinctive opaque color, looked like a magical elixir.

Wow. Maybe people drink 'cause it's all so pretty-looking. Corliss moved to the tray. She poured a little bit out of the martini shaker into the chilled martini glass and brought it up to her nose. She lifted the glass to her mouth and downed what she poured. It tasted awful, like carpet cleaner. But then she began to feel all warm and gooey inside. And suddenly her taste buds were deadened and all she could think was: That's the best carpet cleaner I ever tasted. She poured herself some more and downed that, too. It wasn't helping with the writing, but it was sure helping her forget her writer's block.

Before she knew what she was doing, she'd called JB. "JB!" she shouted into the phone. "It's totally me! Corliss!"

"Hey, girl," came his voice over the other end. "You sure it's you? You sound strange."

"Naw, really? Strange? Me? I'm just happy!"

"Corliss, are you drinking?"

"Whatever do you mean?" said Corliss, quoting Uncle Ross.

"But that's so not like you! And it's not even noon!"

Corliss was licking the bottom of the martini glass. "Yeah, yeah, whatever, listen. I was just sitting here thinking about when your hand was on my knee at Anushka's apartment. Isn't it amazing that I was sitting here thinking that and then I called you and, like, totally said that?"

"Cor, has Uncle Ross been up to no good again?"

"Who? Oh, no. He's great! Listen, you're not gay or anything, are you? Because you like girls a lot, I know, but in a kind of gay way and that would totally bum me out if you were, like, gay." Corliss poured more gin into the martini shaker and shook it up.

"Corliss, I can hear a martini shaker!"

"That? Oh, no, that's not a martini shaker. It's a thing with ice and gin in it and . . . and . . . and . . ." Corliss felt the room swirl around her. Suddenly the ceiling seemed to be moving quickly in her general direction. "Uh-oh, I think I have to—"

And then . . . blackness.

Corliss's Room—Twelve Hours Later

Something thumped repeatedly an inch above Corliss's nose. It took a while, but eventually Corliss realized what was thumping: her head. She started to worry. She couldn't remember anything. Then she squinted and saw before her, lying on its side, a half-empty bottle of Hendrick's Gin. She tried to lift herself off the floor but all the blood rushed to her feet, and she felt the insides of her stomach tumbling around.

When she finally thought to check her watch, she saw that it was almost 11:30 P.M.! She was supposed to have e-mailed Max everything she'd written by 6 P.M. at the latest so he could look it over and make any adjustments before they started shooting the rewrites tomorrow. She tried to do the math to see how many hours late she was, but the addition made her head pound.

Then she remembered something else. Something almost as terrible. *Oh, God. What did I say to JB?* It suddenly came to her. Exactly what she'd said. The full horror of it all. *OH NOOOOOO! I actually brought up Anushka's apartment when his hand was on my knee and then asked him if he liked girls! I AM GOING TO KILL MYSELF NOW! I AM GOING TO LIE DOWN IN TRAFFIC ON SUNSET BOULEVARD AND PRAY FOR A FORD EXPLORER TO ROLL OVER MY CLUELESS BODY!*

Corliss took big breaths and used her hands to pull herself to the bed, where she pressed the intercom to the kitchen.

"Yes, what?" came the chef's curt voice.

"Coffee, please," Corliss croaked.

"I no hear."

"Coffee, dear God, please . . ."

"Oh, coffee. Tsk, tsk. Just like uncle. Drunkie, drunkie,

drunk-drunk." The chef hung up. Corliss summoned every ounce of strength she had to pull herself up to her desk without tossing her tartine. When she got there, she looked down at two and a half pages she'd obviously printed out drunk out of her mind. There were typos and cross-outs and red lines and mysterious notes in indecipherable handwriting. It was a mess.

Corliss was going to kill Uncle Ross. *How dare he show up in my room with enough liquor to choke Lindsay Lohan. What was he thinking! And he made me defer college! I'm sunk. I'm totally and utterly sunk . . .*

She looked down at her phone. There were six new voicemail messages. From the incoming log she could see there were all from *The 'Bu* offices. Max. She didn't have any choice. What she'd written was obviously the drunken ramblings of someone who'd never written a script before, but she had no choice. There was nothing to do, nowhere to turn. They were shooting tomorrow and she had to e-mail it to him.

★ *The 'Bu*

Episode Two
REWRITE BY CORLISS
MEYERS, draft #1

EXT. THE BEACH

It's a really pretty day at the beach.
Seagulls, surfers, and everything.

TRAVIS walks over to his lifeguard stand.
He's really handsome. The handsomest
lifeguard you've ever seen.

                    TRAVIS
          Wow, this day is great. I've
          never seen so many seagulls and
          surfers and everything. But it's
          so perfect today it would suck
          if there were a tragedy in the
          water. That would really bum me
          out.

Travis looks through his BINOCULARS to see
if any tragedy is about to happen.

                    TRAVIS (cont.)
          Looks rad to me. I guess I'll
          just sit up here and flex my
          abs and scope some babes.

OLLIE rushes up the beach, heading for
Travis's lifeguard stand. Ollie looks
really geeky. Like the geekiest guy you've
ever seen.

                        OLLIE
          Travis!

                        TRAVIS
          Don't bother me, Ollie. I'm on
          duty as a lifeguard and you're
          just a geek.

                        OLLIE
          I know you're on duty, Travis!
          That's why I'm here. Because I
          need a lifeguard!

Travis looks at Ollie like, "You are
such a complete and total geek and I'm
embarrassed you're shouting at me."

                    TRAVIS
What is it?

                    OLLIE
It's your ex-girlfriend, Tessa.
She's in trouble!

                    TRAVIS
                 (really mean)
Don't make me laugh. She's
dating Ramone right now. That
Italian guy with all the
muscles. He can worry about
her. Ha!

                    OLLIE
But Ramone is missing! We think
he's been kidnapped by a surfer
gang.

                    TRAVIS
That would serve him right!

                    OLLIE
This is no time for Ramone-
bashing now, Travis. Tessa's
drowning!

Ollie points down the beach to where TESSA
is drowning. Like, really drowning. Not,
like, faking or anything.

                    TESSA
          Help me, I'm drowning! And my
          boyfriend, Ramone, isn't here
          to save me because he's been
          kidnapped by a surfer gang!
          Help! Someone! Anyone!!

Travis gets a real concerned look on his
face. Like he's really worried.

                    TRAVIS
          Hold on, Tessa, I'm coming!

Travis jumps off his lifeguard stand and
dives into the water and rescues Tessa.
It's really dramatic.

                    OLLIE
          Hooray!

Travis carries Tessa to the sand and she
coughs up water and they look at each
other with lovey-dovey eyes.

                    TESSA
          How can I ever thank you,
          Travis? You've saved my life!

                    TRAVIS
          For starters, you can kiss me.

                    TESSA
          I would totally love to do
          that!

They make out. The sun sets. End of scene.

Ten

Max's Limousine—En Route to Malibu—6:45 A.M., the Next Day

"Sweet Scientology . . ." moaned Max to no one in particular, though six of his assistants were in the limo with him hanging on his every word. He was responding to Corliss's script pages, which were so bad, so inept, so talent-free, that they left him breathless.

"What is it, Max?" said the most annoying assistant. This kid had the same spiky haircut as Max, the same Gucci shades, the same Prada pants. He was a veritable mini-Max, and Max usually loved that. But not right now. Right now Max hated his entire life and anyone who reminded him of it. "Is there anything I can do, Max?" said the annoying, identical assistant.

"Not unless you can write a script in the next two hours before the cameras start rolling," said Max, pushing extremely close to his Mariah Carey upper register.

The window between the back of the limo and the front rolled down. "I can write it, Maxth!" came a familiar voice.

"Legend, stop playing with that button and don't give the driver any more directions. I didn't appreciate those twenty minutes we spent lost in that Mar Vista housing complex just now."

"Thorry," said Legend, and the window rolled up.

"Get Corliss on the phone," said Max to his assistants. Immediately, all six of them called Corliss.

"I got her!" said the annoying, mini-Max assistant, giving the other assistants a triumphantly snotty look. He handed over the phone to Max.

"Corliss, this is Max. We've got a problem. Where are you?"

There was a pause on the other end of the line, and then, "Oh, hi, Max. I'm on set. What—what's the problem?"

"I don't want to go into it right now, but let's just say, in regard to the new script you've been working on—we're screwed."

"That bad, huh?" said Corliss, giggling nervously. Max's assistants all made self-satisfied 'I always hated that kiss-ass Corliss' kinds of faces.

"If I'd received it in a timely fashion yesterday, as requested, I might have been able to give you some notes. But as it came late last night—and you know late at night I'm always at some fabulously important dinner—I am only now reading it."

"Max, I don't know what to tell you. I knew this was a bad idea and—"

Max raised his hand in the air. "Corliss, you can't see my hand because we're on the phone, but it's raised in my 'please, cease' gesture and that's what I'd like you to do."

"But Max, I don't know how you could have expected me to—"

"Corliss, I'm hanging up now."

"Okay, Max, we'll talk when you get to the set."

The window between the back and the front seats rolled down again. "Maxth," said Legend. "When we get to Malibu, can I help Tanya put on her thunthcreen like latht time?"

"Legend, what did I say about preschoolers trying to make time with the actresses?"

"It wathn't good?"

Malibu Beach—Twenty Minutes Later

When Max arrived on set, all the production people were in place and ready to roll. The actors were waiting in costumes and makeup. All except Rocco, who was still missing in action. Corliss was there, too, looking abashed. "Still no sign of Mr. DiTullio?" Max asked as he arrived.

"Nothing, Max," said Corliss. "Although there was a strange report on Perez Hilton that said Angelina Jolie was considering adopting him."

Max took a deep breath. "Is that some kind of joke, Corliss?" Corliss nodded meekly. "First of all, you know I'm comedically impaired, so any attempt at humor flies over me like—like—"

"Like something going over your head?"

"Exactly. Second of all, this is no time for jokes. Can I please consult with you a few yards away from these people who are staring at us?" Corliss nodded again.

As they moved away, Max's assistants gave Corliss a

look that said, *You're in trouble*. "Pay no attention to their evil little faces, Corliss," said Max. "You know you're worth more to me than all of them combined."

Corliss looked at him in complete disbelief. "That's sweet, Max, but I've totally let you down. The script I e-mailed you is terrible, you're right. I wouldn't use it to paper Uncle Ross's cockatoo cage!"

"Corliss, you're correct. The script is unspeakably bad." He shook it in the air. "Rocco's character was kidnapped by a surfer gang? Do surfers even *have* gangs?"

"Um, I think I read somewhere that they do . . ."

"And the dialogue, Corliss. *Oy*, as Michael Rothstein would say. It's as wooden as my Prada shoe trees."

"That bad, huh?"

"I've heard more expressive dialogue coming out of Legend on the monkey bars. In fact, I might as well have offered him the rewrite job! Or offered it to some valet at the Grove. Or to that dumb-dumb cashier at that Rite Aid on Sunset. Or to six brain-damaged orangutans with typewriters."

"Um, a little harsh?"

"Sorry, but the thing is, we're in a quagmire."

"Good word."

"Thanks, Adam Levine used it on the phone with me last night. We're developing a movie where he plays a meth-addicted go-go boy, and we're negotiating the nudity. He wants full frontal, but I only want a few butt shots."

"Wow, sounds tough."

"It's terrible, lawyers are making tens of thousands of dollars as we speak trying to solve it. But Adam Levine's *derriere* has nothing to do with *our* quagmire, which is, basically, that we're screwed. We have no script to shoot, we're still missing one of our lead actors, and the well is being *constantly poisoned* by secrets from that freakin' blog! Secrets that keep erupting like—like—"

"Exploding secrets?"

"Exactly. My nerves are shot, my Xanax prescription has run out, and my Scientology counselor has taken a part-time job as Oprah's L.A. gardener, which means her hours devoted to *me* are cut in half!"

"Ouch."

"To top it off, if we don't get a script shot this week, there will not BE a second episode of *The 'Bu*, which is unthinkable for a show that's a huge hit. I will be fired, which means everyone will be fired—that's in my contract. So, no, it's not a good day, Corliss, and I think we need to start with a clean slate."

"This is terrible. What do you have in mind, Max?"

Max took a moment to strategize. "First, we need to push back production a day or two, and you need to take a crack at another draft."

"But Max!"

"I will help you this time, Corliss, but we need *something* halfway decent on paper. Look at the old scripts, for heaven's sake."

"Okay, but—"

"And while that's happening, before any of us take one more step, we need a *cleansing*. The reason we're in this mess is because Rocco was keeping a huge secret. And the reason we've had so many other problems is because of *all the other secrets*."

"Secrets revealed on The 'Bu-hoo."

"Exactly. I need to know everything I'm dealing with here. Everyone's dark corners—including yours, Corliss Meyers."

"But I don't have any dark corners, Max! I mean, I barely have corners," she said, looking down at her body.

"That may be, but in ten minutes I want the cast assembled, slathered with SPF 90, and ready to spill. I don't want to be caught off guard anymore by what I read online. I want confessions and I want them *now*. This will give you some time to do rewrites."

"But Max, seriously. I don't—"

"Corliss, my 'please cease' hand is poised to raise itself."

Corliss looked at her feet. "Okay, I'll do my best, Max. I'll assemble the cast in the catering tent and then," she took a big breath, "take a crack at another draft."

"Borrow the laptop in my trailer, Corliss. And if you need anything, don't hesitate to ask one of my junior assistants for it. They may loathe you because of your seniority, but they'll do whatever research, printing, or collating you need."

"Thanks, Max. I'll assemble the cast in the catering tent, and then I'll head to your trailer to work on those rewrites."

"Excellent. I'll want to see what you've got by 3:30 this afternoon, no later. Come to my trailer and knock three quick knocks on the door, followed by two slow knocks."

Corliss saluted and dashed off, spraying sand behind her. Max sent up a silent prayer to L. Ron Hubbard.

The Catering Tent—Fifteen Minutes Later

The cast and production crew were assembled. Trent looked longingly at a tray of doughnuts. Tanya clutched the tiny crucifix she wore as a necklace. JB was attempting some crunches, but he soon gave up.

"People," Max said as his assistants lined up behind him like a security detail. "Today's script is undergoing a last-minute rewrite."

Everyone groaned.

"Nothing to worry about. It will be fine-tuned and perfect by this afternoon."

"Can I get some stock options on that?" JB said, grinning. Everyone laughed.

"Please, there will be no laughter now!" said Max. "I want to talk about something serious while we're waiting for the script."

Everyone rolled their eyes.

"No eye-rolling! We have a bigger problem. A problem of *morale*. And it's all because of that blog—The 'Bu-hoo."

Now everyone snapped to attention. Max had never brought up the blog to anyone but Corliss. The cast leaned forward. The production crew looked blank—but they always did. Max dove in.

"It seems that every few days the person who is writing that despicable blog reveals another secret that cripples us like—like—" He looked around for Corliss to help him with the metaphor.

Tanya raised her hand. "Like a crippled person?"

"Something like that, yes. And these secrets have slowed us down, contributed to a drastic writing-staff reduction, and in one very prominent case, driven one of our stars from our very bosom."

JB giggled. "Sorry! 'Bosom' gets me every time."

Max ignored JB. He wanted them to know he meant business. "I can't risk any more calamities because of that blog. I'm trying to find out who is behind it, but until that time, I need to know, right here and in front of everyone, if there are any more secrets I should be aware of before they come out."

No one said a word. Tanya looked at Trent who looked at JB who looked at Tanya. Then Tanya looked at JB who looked at Trent. Finally Tanya raised her hand.

"I made out with Trent at the premiere party!" she yelped. "But only for old time's sake!"

"Hey," said Trent. "I thought that mack session meant we were getting back together."

"Bwa-ha-haa!" said JB in his Dracula voice. "She's got you in her clutches!"

Max sighed. "Thank you, Tanya, but that hardly qualifies as a dark secret. You apparently made out with half the people at that party, or at least that's what I heard through the grapevine."

"She did?" said Trent, looking all hurt.

Tanya applauded and laughed. "I love the grapevine!"

"Now listen to me, people," said Max in his most resonant whisper. "We have to go *deeper*. I want the *deepest, darkest dirt* you have. This is your opportunity to purge your souls. We are all friends here, we've been through a lot together, we already know a lot about each other—there's no reason to hold anything back. Especially when the very success of *The 'Bu* is at stake. I beg of you, I implore you. I'll even buy you whatever you want at the Prada store in Beverly Hills. I just want to know everything I don't know about you yet—before it comes out online to bite us in our collective butts."

Tanya, Trent, and JB's eyes were as big as saucers. Finally, Tanya raised her hand again. Her lips quivered and her chest heaved. "Yes, Tanya," said Max. "What is it?"

"Yeah," said Trent, looking worried. "What is it?"

"Yeah!" grinned JB, bobbing up and down. "Tell, tell!"

"Well, it's kinda hard to tell with everyone looking all googly-eyed at me. But if I can change my top in front of all those *Sports Illustrated* photographers, I guess I can do this."

Max looked at her solemnly. "It's for the good of *The 'Bu*, Tanya."

"Okay, then," she said. "The thing is—oh, boy, Jesus is going to be really mad at me for this . . ."

"Don't worry, Tanya," said Max, moving to her with some pamphlets one of his assistants always carried. "You can always become a Scientologist. Read these and get back to me."

"Thanks, Max," she said, taking a pamphlet. "Okay, the thing is . . . my big secret . . ."

Everyone leaned in. Even the production people.

"My biggest secret ever is that I'm not, like, virgin-y." She closed her eyes before she went on. "I'm like *totally not* virgin-y. I'm—I'm—I'm, like, a person who's *totally lost their virginity.*"

Trent's eyes flew open as big as boogie boards. JB's mouth hung to his chest.

"Well, Tanya," said Max, not expecting this particular

secret. "I appreciate your candor and—"

"I mean, like, I was a complete and total slut all through high school. They called me Slutty LaSlut."

JB fell over in the sand. Trent had to reach for a beach chair.

"I mean, I did, like, everyone in school, and everyone at Home Depot, where I worked until I was discovered as a model."

"You mean everyone as in *everyone*?" wailed Trent.

"Numbers!" said JB. "I want numbers!"

"Even everyone at *Home Depot*?" whimpered Trent. "Like, even the guys in the garden department?"

"Yes, even them! And then I became a model and did all the male models I met! And then I heard about the job on *The 'Bu*. And I prayed so hard to Jesus about it because I wanted it *so bad*. And then Jesus totally heard my prayers, and I got cast! So I was like, 'I better turn over a new leaf for Jesus and stop being so easy.' So that's how I thanked Jesus for the job on this show. By pretending to be a virgin all over again!"

"Great," said Max, whose breath got labored as he realized he'd just set in motion something terrible, awful. Something catastrophically stupid. *I've assembled everyone to spill their secrets so that I won't be caught off guard anymore when they appear online, but the person writing that blog could be in this very tent! And they could head off after this meeting and tell the world!* "Okay, thank you everyone. Meeting over."

A round of confused looks was followed by a chorus of "What?" and "Why?"

"Did you want a bigger secret?" asked Tanya. "I could

give you, like, the list of names. I have it in my trailer. One of the Home Depot guys went on to become very big in the fertilizing business."

"No!" shouted Max. "But thanks for sharing." He looked around for Corliss to help him out of the giant hole he had just dug himself. Then he remembered she was off doing rewrites. "Where is the PR person? I need the PR person!" Max's assistants scattered to find the PR person. The cast gave him a strange look. "It's nothing, I've, um, just realized our personal lives should, um, remain personal, and they have nothing whatsoever to do with *The 'Bu* and if anyone decides to write about them online, for instance, then we will just have to—just have to—"

Max's assistants returned with the PR person, Brayden, a strange-looking young man who wore a rhinestone-studded BCBG baseball cap and an American Apparel muscle T. "You wanted me, Max?"

"Yes, Brayden, we need to confab. All hell is breaking loose—"

"Yeah," said Tanya, with an uncharacteristically stern look on her face. "I just told everyone I wasn't a virgin and now I think I feel all icky about it."

"Well, I don't!" said JB.

"Well, I do," said Trent. "It's nobody's business!"

"It's *my* business," said Tanya. "So it's *somebody's* business, Trent."

"I'm trying to, like, protect you!" Trent shot back.

"Another day on *The 'Bu*," said JB, sighing. "Not much work on the show, but there sure is a lot of drama!"

"Bring it way down, people!" barked Brayden. "This is

exactly the kind of stuff that keeps leaking out to the press, and I want everyone to put a big, fat pin in it." Brayden was baring his impossibly white teeth like a rabid dog. Max shrank when he saw them, then tried to sneak out, waving to his assistants to follow him. "You're not going anywhere, Max. Not until we figure out this PR nightmare once and for all!"

Somewhere on the Coast—Noon

The Bu-Hoo

It's SO easy!!!!! It's like shooting goldfish in a dog-food bowl! Those adorable 'Bu tykes can't stop talking!

KEY PHRASE: THE LAST ONE GOES DOWN

Here it is, kiddies. (And Jesus is going to be *soooooo* disappointed!) Tanya Ventura, the gal who gave Trent Owen Michaels blue balls for four straight months, is . . .

1★) A COMPLETE AND TOTAL FORMER
   SLUTSKY
2★) DE-VIRGINFIED AS OF YEARS AGO
3★) A BIG DUMB-DUMB BLABBERMOUTH

All true! How do I know, you ask? MBK knows all. But I wouldn't have known if the skinny Latina hadn't blurted it out HERSELF. For once I was totally out of the loop. Tanya "lack of V" Ventura totally did herself in completely on her own.

DONCHA LOVE IT?? All MBK has to do these days is sit down, put my feet up, and wait for all the dirty dirt to come to me!

But hold yer horses, hornsters! Don't go knocking on Ms. Ventura's trailer door any time soon. She claims they're bolted shut for business now that she's a big star. Some kind of deal she made with the guy upstairs—that there would be no guy downstairs, *if you catch my drift.*
Me so bad. ME! ME! ME!

And if it all weren't so effing delicious already, it looks like the cast is turning on M2 all over again!

It was only a matter of time. He's TOTALLY out of control, totally being abandoned by everyone around him. He's on a crash course to out-of-the-picture-ville. Why does that make MBK *soooooo* happy??

Love and all things *'Bu*,
MBK

Max's Trailer—3:30 P.M.

The sun was high in the sky as Corliss approached the trailer. She could see Max sitting inside at his desk. She had the rewrites, which she'd been working on all day, in her hands. She was convinced they were so much better than the rewrites she'd given Max the day before. In fact, she thought they were pretty darn good. Maybe not brilliant, but certainly a solid second draft.

Of course, she had *some* doubts about what she'd written, but she ignored all the skeptical voices in her head (except for the one that kept asking her if she might be schizophrenic) and soldiered on, up the stairs to Max's trailer. She knocked three quick knocks on the door, followed by two slow knocks. But Max didn't say, "Come in."

She mushed her face up against the door and whispered, "Max, it's me, Corliss. I just did the knock."

But still, she heard nothing. She craned her neck to look inside to see if she had imagined seeing Max at his desk. *I'm completely strung out and that's often when people have hallucinatory experiences*, she thought. But, sure enough, Max was inside at his desk. Corliss knocked on the window.

"Max, it's me!"

Max finally looked up. He seemed like he didn't recognize her.

"It's Corliss! I need to come in. Is that okay?"

He nodded slowly, and she entered the trailer. It was a complete mess inside. Scripts were everywhere, paper was shredded to bits, magazines were scattered about, Prada shoe trees hung from lampshades.

"Max, my God, what happened? It's usually perfect in here. Now it looks like one of those white-trash trailers on *COPS*. Was there a break-in? Are you okay?"

Max took a breath and finally spoke. "I think I'm having a nervous breakdown. You might know a more clinical term for it, but it's the thing that happens when your nerves finally give out and you start to cry and your hair starts to look really bad because you've been pulling it out of your head."

Corliss rushed to him. "Max, talk to me! What can I do? Are you okay? And I never thought I'd suggest this, but should I call your Scientology counselor?"

"As of this morning, I no longer have a Scientology counselor. She wants to work full-time pruning Oprah's rosebushes. She says it's half the hours, twice the pay, and 100 percent less aggravation. Can you believe, on this day of all days, my Scientology counselor dumps me for Oprah's roses?"

Corliss's empathy kicked in. She knew this was a catastrophe for Max. She had to proceed delicately and speak in soothing tones. "That's terrible, Max. Listen, come over here to the leather sofa, lie down so you're comfortable, and tell me as much as you can remember."

Max moved to the sofa and stretched out. Corliss picked up a pen and pad from the floor and pulled up a chair.

"Do we have to go back to my childhood?"

"No, Max, just start from today."

"First of all, how much do you charge?"

"Max, please, I'm not even a freshman in college yet so this is completely free—and just between you and me."

"Okay, Corliss. What happened is this. I asked the cast about secrets I wasn't yet aware of, and in the middle of Tanya spilling her heart out I realized I was a total idiot and called Brayden, *The 'Bu* PR person, about the nightmare that was about to unfold."

"Seeking help is a sign of a healthy mind, Max."

"Thank you. But then it goes from bad to worse. Brayden came by to talk to the cast and crew, and now my assistants tell me they're all in the catering tent having a total meltdown about how unprofessional the set is, how I don't know what I'm doing, and how I'm more concerned with my own physical appearance than with making a good TV show." Max shot up on the sofa to look at himself in his big mirror. "My physical appearance is excellent, why should I be concerned about it?"

"Er—"

Max lay back down. "And then, to comfort myself while I was being torn to shreds behind my back by my very own cast and crew, I signed on to get my e-mail—my mother e-mails me every Thursday about how brilliant I am—and once I was online I couldn't help opening The 'Bu-hoo."

Corliss shook her head. "Max . . ."

"Don't say it, you're right. But there, in lurid prose, I read about the cast meeting I'd just left! And how Tanya was, before coming to Hollywood, practically a panty-less wonder."

"What?!"

Max nodded and closed his eyes. "Then it starts to get murky, Corliss. But I remember Michael Rothstein called. He'd just received a call himself from some big organization called something like People for a Sex-Free America. They're one of those family values watchdog groups. The kind that watches other people's families and judges them on their behavior."

"Uh-oh." Corliss had a premonition about what Max was about to tell her.

"Anyway, this group of sex-free people told Michael Rothstein they were organizing a massive boycott of the next 'Bu episode! Because all of the cast members are degenerates! Michael says this group has real power, and wanted to know what I was going to do about it."

It was just as Corliss predicted. The 'Bu was becoming a cultural phenomenon after one episode! It was now vulnerable to attacks from all corners. "But there's nothing you can do about it, Max. Some things are out of our control, remember?"

"Don't try to console me with your psychiatric platitudes, Corliss. I know!"

"Well, jeez, you don't have to be so—"

"So then Michael says, 'And where's Rocco?' and I say, 'The last rumor that crossed my desk was that he was hiding out in some cave in Tora Bora!' Which made Michael really, um, cranky, and he threatened to fire me. And then he asked me why we haven't found out who is writing The 'Bu-hoo by now! And I said, 'Because all our time and energy has been put into the rewrite for the second episode!' Do you have it by the way, Corliss?"

"I do, Max, and I think I've really made great strides." She handed him the rewrite.

Max took a moment to look over a few pages and then wailed like a stuck pig. "Corliss, we're doomed! This is the most execrable writing I've ever seen!"

"What?!" Corliss's mind reeled. "Doesn't *execrable* mean *sucky*? It can't be sucky! I worked really hard on that Max! I even consulted with Uncle Ross on a few parts!" Bits of Corliss's life started to flash before her eyes. And then *she* started to have a nervous breakdown. "I deferred college for a whole semester! My mother isn't speaking to me! I've spent the last two days sleepless, drunk, and losing my mind! And for what?! To go crazy trying to do yet another job for you that I have zilch qualifications for?"

Max put his hands over his eyes. "It's all going dark again, Corliss! My life is ending! Your life is obviously over, too!"

Corliss took a big breath. She realized that two people losing their minds simultaneously wouldn't solve anything. "Max, listen. We just have to think! You and I have been a pretty great team. We're at our best at moments of crisis. And if this isn't a crisis, I don't know what is."

"It certainly is that, Corliss!" Max trilled in his soprano register. "It's so bad I don't care if I sound like Christina Aguilera on helium! We're screwed!"

Corliss put her fingers in her ears in case Max was going to keep shouting in his girly voice. She thought as hard as she could, summoning every inner resource she had. Then it came to her, wrapped in red ribbons and glowing like Christmas. "Max, Max, Max! I might have the beginnings of one of my off-kilter but strangely viable ideas. What did you say Brayden the PR person is doing?"

"He's in the catering tent encouraging the cast to tear me and the show apart."

"Exactly! That gives me an idea."

"It does?" Max sat straight up.

Corliss's mind was alive, firing on all pistons. An idea was coming to her slowly. An amazing idea, surrounded by sparkles and fireworks. She wanted to sell Max on it, but she knew she'd have to deliver it in bite-sized chunks. He was dancing too close to the crazy brink to absorb too much at once. She had to spell it out carefully. "Okay, *The 'Bu* is not a reality television show, right?"

"Of course it isn't."

"But reality TV is *really big* right now, right?"

Max looked confused. "Corliss, I don't—"

"Listen, Max. We're in a bind because we don't have a second episode because I'm inept as a writer."

"You're the worst!"

"You don't have to be so emphatic about it."

"Sorry."

"No worries. So, okay, since we don't have a good *script*, what if we did the second *'Bu* show . . . *live*?"

Max looked even more confused. "Live? But how? What do you mean?" He rolled his fingers for her to explain quickly.

"Hear me out, Max. Since there's so much turmoil on the show, and everyone in America has been reading about it on The 'Bu-hoo, why don't we air our dirty laundry live on television?"

"I don't get you, Corliss. Are *you* having a breakdown?"

"I was, but now I'm back. And I know it sounds crazy, but it's just the kind of crazy that might work. Since the actors have become famous because of their antics *off television*, why don't we have, like, a kind of group therapy session with all of them *on television*? They can talk about how hard it is to be young and in Hollywood, *blah, blah,* and then they can say how *really sorry* they are for behaving so poorly—which would be fascinating television, and would shut up those not-so-sexy family values people at the same time, y'know? And we shoot the whole thing in front of an audience full of real teens asking real questions! Kind of like Dr. Phil meets MTV's *Total Request Live*. Whaddya think?"

Max looked like he was beginning to understand. "But Corliss, will people actually watch? After all, the American public doesn't know the cast members very well yet. Only one 'Bu show has aired. The American public might be licking their lips over a few sentences in a blog every day, but will they tune into an *entire show* about our cast's personal problems?"

"Good point, good point. Let me think." Corliss concentrated as hard as she could as thoughts flashed through her head, some not so bad, some completely lame. Then she had it. An amaaaaaazing idea. Something that could put this live 'Bu TV show over the top. Something *irresistible*. "What if we ask Anushka to make a special guest appearance?"

"What?"

"Yes, Max! Think about it. She's a big star. No matter what *you* think of her, America can't get enough of her. They will for sure tune in to watch Anushka Peters apologize for her bad behavior."

Max scowled. "Yes, and totally trash me in the process."

Corliss hadn't thought of that. "Well, we'll just tell her she can't do that!"

"No, wait, Corliss." Max's face lit up. "That is exactly what Anushka *should* do. Her coming on the show to totally trash me could stir up SO much publicity AND buy us time for someone—but of course not *you*—to write a second episode."

"Of course," Corliss said, swallowing her pride.

"Listen, if you can convince Anushka to come on the show, it will be *brilliant* television. Just think of it: all of our actors interacting with real teens in a real live audience, spilling their guts, baring their souls—and asking America's forgiveness in the process! It not only has the makings of the teen television event of a lifetime, it's also an opportunity for us to thumb our noses at The 'Bu-hoo!"

"But how? What do you mean?"

"Corliss! Don't you see? We won't have to worry about finding out who MBK is anymore, because once the live episode airs there won't be any more secrets for MBK to uncover! You're brilliant! I'm brilliant! We're brilliant!"

"My God, we are!" Corliss felt herself blush. It was thrilling to hear Max use the same adjective to describe them both. *Brilliant!* It meant that even if her writing skills weren't all that, her ascent up the Hollywood food chain wasn't doomed.

She still had a future as a producer—and they were the real idea people, after all. And if the plan worked, she wouldn't have to snoop around trying to find out who MBK was anymore! Corliss suddenly felt lighter than Indiana whipped cream.

"Of course, Michael Rothstein and the network will have to approve," Max continued. "But I think if I finally give Mingmei that shoulder rub she's been asking for, she might put in a good word."

"Now you're thinking!"

"Corliss, this therapy session has been remarkable. Next session can I tell you about wetting my undies in second grade?"

"Um, maybe, Max. But let's concentrate on saving *The 'Bu* first."

"Good idea. What will I do without you?"

"Well, I deferred school for a semester, so you're kinda stuck with me for the next five months."

Max lit up like Christmas. "Corliss, were you *serious* about that? You're really staying? That's wonderful! And we can continue talking about it in a celebratory fashion once the state of our show is less precarious, but for now we've got work to do! Go to the catering tent and convince the cast of your brilliant plan, then run this by Anushka. In the meantime, I'll get on the horn to Mingmei Rothstein and ask if she's got forty-five minutes and a massage table. Let's see if we can't turn this lemon into something we can drink!"

Corliss dashed for the door. "I'm off like a prom dress!"

Max raised an eyebrow.

"Well, not *my* prom dress. I didn't go to my prom. And

if I had, my prom dress would have only come off when I got back home."

"TMI, Corliss, TMI!"

Outside Max's Trailer—Twelve Minutes Later

Corliss was breathless as she waited for Anushka to answer her phone. Finally, She of the Husky Voice picked up.

"Cor, what up?"

"Anushka, you're not going to believe it. Where are you? Are you sitting down?"

"Girl, I am *lying* down. I'm at Burke Williams with 'magic hands' Rudolf, getting one of the best massages of my life."

"Well, don't let the towel slip off when you hear what I'm about to say."

"What towel?"

"Never mind, listen. It's completely whacko what's going on. And this idea is totally nuts but in a totally brilliant way, if I do say so myself, and—"

"Cor, Cor, I am *way* mellow here and you're charting really high on the strung-out meter."

"Sorry." Corliss composed herself. "The thing is—the thing is—"

"Spit it out, *Chiquita*."

"The thing is, Max wants you back!"

"WHAT?"

"Okay, but listen. It's a one-show only deal. And it's going to be live."

"LIVE?"

"I don't want to explain it on the phone, Anushka. Can you

come to the beach to talk to Max and hammer out the details?" Anushka didn't answer. "Anushka? Hello? *Anushka?*"

And click went the line, as Anushka—Corliss could only assume, anyway—raced to the set of *The 'Bu*.

Max's Trailer—Fifty-Seven Minutes Later

The ball was in Anushka's court. Both Max and Corliss had spent the last five minutes begging her to appear on the live broadcast of *The 'Bu*. Max had even kneeled down at one point. Anushka hadn't answered them. Mostly because she wanted to see Max sweat through his Ermenegildo Zegna shirt. She leaned forward and rested her chin on her knuckles. "And I can say *anything* I want on this live show?"

Max looked at Corliss. Corliss nodded. "Yes, Anushka," said Max. "*Anything.*"

"See?" said Corliss to Anushka. "I told you Max would be accommodating. The only thing we would like you to say is that you realize you are a role model to young people and that you take that role seriously. If you can manage to do that without laughing."

Anushka sat back in her chair and slowly crossed and uncrossed her magnificent legs as Max chewed his Montblanc fountain pen to smithereens. "Okay," she said finally. "I'll do it." Max and Corliss leaped from their seats. "On two conditions." Max and Corliss sank back into their seats. "First condition: That I come back on the show not just for this live episode, but for *the rest of the season*." Max leaped out of his seat again. "Second: That when I *do* come back on the show for the rest of the season, the writers have to make my every move *hot*.

I want to dress hot, talk hot, act hot, be hot. HOT, HOT, HOT. Whaddya say?"

Corliss tugged Max back down to his seat, and then gestured to him to take some deep breaths. "All right, Anushka," he began once he felt a little calmer. "But I'm still the director. You can come back to *The 'Bu*, and I will make sure you are 'hot,' but I am still *and always* the one in charge."

"Of course, Max," Anushka said in her devilish voice. "I swear I'll be good."

"Of course she will be, Max," said Corliss. "She's a whole new Anushka! Isn't that right?"

"Totally," said Anushka, standing up and heading for the door. "So when is this live show, anyway, and what do I have to do to prepare?"

"It's one week from tonight, Anushka," said Corliss. "And all we want you to do is be yourself. Isn't that right, Max?"

Max gulped.

UBC Network—a Soundstage—One Week Later—8:12 P.M.

Tanya, Trent, and JB were assembled in big, comfy chairs in a row across the stage, with tiny microphones clipped to their clothes. Max and Corliss sat on the stage, too, and behind them, on risers, sat *The 'Bu* production crew.

The entire group faced an audience of teens, who bounced up and down in their chairs from the excitement of being so close to people they'd seen on TV just one week before. They'd been asking the actors about how fabulous it was being on a new hit show, and the actors had been graciously telling them.

"And were you all, like, totally stoked when you got the call that you were on the show?" asked someone in the front row.

"I was totally stoked," said Trent. "I was all like 'whoa, no way' about it."

Someone a few rows back jumped up with his hand in the air. "This is a question for Tanya. How do you stay so smokin'?"

"Awww," said Tanya. "That's sooo cute of you to ask. Basically I use a lot of face products. And body products. So my face and my body have a lot of products on them is my answer to your question."

Corliss could sense the show had been pretty smooth sailing so far, but things were about to get dicey—which is what needed to happen for this live 'Bu event to come off.

Max stood and addressed the teens in the audience. "Thanks everyone. Your questions have been great so far. And now I'd like to introduce someone very special to all of us. Someone who will no doubt spice things up in her own special way. Please give a warm welcome to . . . Anushka Peters!"

The place went nuts. The audience leaped to its feet. Anushka strode out from behind a curtain in a flouncy, sleeveless Moschino cocktail dress, looking like heaven on heels. She lifted her hands to stop the cheers.

"Please," she said in the strange British diction she used in public. "You are too kind!"

She took a comfy seat next to Tanya, who held her hand. Corliss knew the real show was about to begin.

Max turned to the audience. "Many of you saw Anushka's character Samantha die a fiery death in the pilot episode. Are there any questions for her now that we've brought her back to life?"

The audience laughed and cheered and Anushka waved like the Queen.

"Third-degree burns, but I'm here! But before we begin, I would like to say something serious." The audience leaned forward. "A lot has been written about me, some of it good, some of it bad. I just want to say to America," she spread her arms wide, "that I am truly sorry if I have disappointed you. I realize I am *an idol* to literally *millions and millions* of people. And from here on out I have only one goal: to be a lean, clean, actin' machine!" The crowd cheered.

"And *I'd* like to say something, too," shouted Tanya over the din. The audience quieted and watched intently as Tanya dabbed at the corners of her eyes with a tissue. "Some things have been written about *me*, too. Things that are, like, really sucky. But I just want America to know that I am *not* Slutty LaSlut." The audience gasped. "I am Tanya Ventura, a good Catholic girl. Hi, Mom and Dad!" She waved at the camera and smiled, before growing serious again. "Sure, maybe I did do everyone at Home Depot when I worked there." The audience gasped again. "But that doesn't mean I was a bad person. It just means I was a little loose in my lady cha-cha."

Corliss couldn't believe it. The audience was lapping up every word! Her whole body tingled. She sensed TVs across the country being flicked on as people called each other about the show. She looked over at Max, who could barely contain his glee.

"*But*," Tanya continued, "I just want to say that I am *totally* re-virginized since I got the part on *The 'Bu*, and that

I'm saving myself for marriage."

"Yeah!" said Anushka, holding Tanya's hand in the air. "So what if Tanya and I have been passed around like nuts at Christmas? Ha! We're just a couple of teenage girls trying to bust out every once in a while!"

"Yeah!" said JB, jumping to his feet and shoving his scrawny fist in the air. "And I for one can tell you that these two fair ladies *never* judged me for abusing my mom's credit card online!" The audience howled and hollered.

"We wouldn't *ever* do that, JB," said Tanya, her chest heaving with sobs. "And we also know you aren't just some creepy guy who steals my nipple Band-Aids to sell on eBay. You're *totally more* than that!"

"And another thing!" said Anushka. "I think I speak for Tanya when I say JB is the kind of guy we would go to immediately if we were ever hurt . . . or sad . . . or upset . . . or even in jail! *He is totally that guy!*"

JB's lower lip quivered at the tribute. "You two are like sisters to me! And I never had sisters, or a real family who believed in me, even." Corliss saw JB as if for the first time: authentic, honest, and so sad.

"I didn't have a family like that, either," said Anushka, suddenly serious. "We lived above a deli, and kids teased me because I always smelled like pickles. And my mom said there were worse things to smell like! Never, 'I love you' or 'I believe in you.' But you guys believe in me," she said as a single tear rolled down her cheek.

"We do!" wailed Tanya, now a puddle of tears. "And we love you, too!"

"We do!" said JB, struggling not to cry. "You're like—like

my family," he managed, finally bursting into tears. Tanya ran to him and hugged him so hard his eyes bugged out of his head. The audience went into convulsions.

"Like, what about me?" said Trent, looking put out. "Don't I get to express my, like, feelings and apologize for stuff?" Anushka, Tanya, and Trent nodded at him encouragingly, and he stepped forward. "Okay." He looked at his feet and blinked. The audience sat forward in their seats. "So, like, the thing I'd like to apologize for is for, like, not being the kind of low-carb stud who could get Tanya back." Now *his* chest started to heave. "Because I really, really like her."

Corliss's jaw hung open in astonishment. The crowd was going nuts. The four castmates were in tears, and they weren't acting. She watched as they moved together in a group hug, crying and wiping each other's faces as the crowd went through the roof, stomping and leaping onto their chairs and throwing their arms in the air. And then, just when Corliss thought the din couldn't get any louder, a howl rose from the audience. She looked around to see the source of the commotion. It was Rocco, emerging from stage left, looking tan and gorgeous.

"Ladies and gentleman," called Max. "It's Rocco DiTullio!"

The crying mass of hugging 'Bu castmates ran to Rocco and embraced him in another group hug as the crowd chanted. "'Bu forever, 'Bu forever!" Finally, Rocco broke from the others and quieted down the crowd.

"I would just like to add one thing to the chorus of brave admissions today. And that is that Tanya, Anushka, Trent, and especially JB, are some of the best people I know. We're young, so we don't always know how we should proceed with our lives. We make mistakes, just like all of you. And just like all of you, we ask that our trials and tribulations be considered private."

The audience stood as one and cheered so loudly Corliss thought the roof would fly off the soundstage. The cast held each other and wept. The sight should have made her happy, but she suddenly felt so sad. As much as all of them had made her feel a part of things, Corliss realized, looking at them all huddled together now, that no matter how creative or smart or helpful they were, no matter how many brilliant ideas they had, no matter how many friendships they cultivated, people like Max and her were always going to be on the *outside* looking *in*.

Uncle Ross's Pool—9:20 A.M., the Next Morning

Corliss wanted to dive into the koi pond and stay underwater forever. Her mood had been heading south since the show the night before, and no matter what she did she wasn't able to pull herself up.

"Corliss," said Uncle Ross, scurrying across the lanai in his cashmere Armani bathrobe. "I watched the live 'Bu broadcast last night, and it was the most brilliant television I have ever seen."

"Glad you liked it," said Corliss as she lobbed a pebble into the koi pond.

"Liked it? I loved it! All the morning trades are clamoring about the ratings it pulled down—the most watched show this week. Aren't you excited?"

"I should be, Uncle Ross. It's great news. *And* Max just

called to say Michael Rothstein doesn't care about the blog anymore now that everything's out in the open. So I don't have to keep snooping to find out who the mysterious MBK is."

"Lovely. But then what's with the frowny face, my darling?"

"I don't know, Uncle Ross. I just looked at the cast last night and realized they *belong* to something. They have each other. Sure I hang out with them sometimes, and I've gotten pretty close to Anushka and JB, but at the end of the day I'm just the director's assistant. I don't really belong to anything."

"Oh, Corliss, if it makes any difference, I'm certain the cast doesn't think that way."

"I bet they do. You're just saying that to be nice, Uncle Ross."

"Oh, my dear, dear Corliss. Haven't you realized by now that I never do anything just to be nice?" Then Uncle Ross extended his arm, game show hostess-style. "Exhibit A: your cast, standing in the foyer, waiting to talk to you."

Corliss jumped to her feet. "What?"

Uncle Ross called into the house. "Come on now, kiddies. We're back here by the pool. Go past the statue of the naked discus thrower, make a left at the statue of the naked shot put champion, and continue on until you come to the naked triathlete just kind of standing there."

Tanya and Trent appeared first. JB followed with Rocco and, pulling up the rear as usual, was Anushka, dressed down in a cute American Apparel halter and Diesel jean short-shorts.

"Hey, kid," said Anushka in her husky, non-British real voice. "We've all got something to say to you."

Corliss couldn't imagine what.

"Yeah," said Tanya.

"Like, yeah," said Trent.

"First of all," said Rocco, stepping forward. "I want to profess my appreciation."

"You do? To *me*?"

"I talked to Max before the broadcast last night, and he showed me all your notes about trying to track me down in Sicily. I was really moved that you'd go to all that trouble to help out *The 'Bu*. It shows a real commitment on your part. I never should have left without informing the staff, and you suffered a lot to find me. You were professional, Corliss, and I wasn't. *Mea culpa*."

Corliss was touched by this unexpected tribute. "You were under the pull of an addiction, Rocco! We were all worried."

"I'm better now, thank you. I'm in Steroids Anonymous and my sponsor happens to be someone I've looked up to and admired for a long time now."

"Rocco is saying no to 'roids," said Trent.

"I'm really glad to hear that," said Corliss. "Good for you, Rocco."

"Yup," said JB. "We're all on the road to righteousness—yes!" He pumped his scrawny fist in the air. "And you know what else, Ms. Meyers? I feel two tons o' better after coming clean on national TV last night. It's like a giant stone has been lifted from my sunken chest. Hey! It occurs to me maybe that's why my chest is sunken in the first place."

"And another thing, Corliss," said Tanya. "Seeing Trent talk about how he wasn't a big enough stud to get me back really made me sad—and then it got me totally hot for him again.

So now we're back together!" Tanya jumped up and down and clapped.

"Which means," said Trent, grinning like the cat who ate the canary, "I'm way off the carbs and, like, totally sticking to my diet and *totally* amping up the crunches. Gots to keep tight for Tans!"

"And I'm letting him call me Tans now!" yelped Tanya, clapping even more.

"That's awesome, you two," said Corliss.

"Of course," Tanya continued, "I've still promised Jesus no one's getting a piece of this till I'm walking down the aisle, but at least everything's out in the open between me and Trent. Now we're all over each other like yellow on rice. That's a Puerto Rican phrase that means we're, like, totally all over each other."

"I'm really glad, Tanya. You two always looked great all over each other."

Tanya jumped up and down and clapped, and then she and Trent made out in front of everyone to prove how great they looked all over each other.

"Get a room," said Anushka, laughing. "But the really big news, Cor, is that after my appearance on the show last night I've been offered—get this—my own reality show. How cool is that? They are going to drop me in the Brazilian rain forest for two weeks and see if I can live among the indigenous reptile population."

"Go, Anushka!" said Corliss. "You'll be great with reptiles!"

"Right?" agreed Anushka. "Me? Snakes? We *totally* go together."

"But what about your part on *The 'Bu*?" asked Corliss.

"Don't worry, kid," said Anushka. "My new managers and agents assure me I can do both. I'm becoming a *brand*. And that's a good thing!"

"I don't believe it," said Corliss, looking around at everyone. "You mean all these good things came out of last night's show?"

Everyone nodded. "And we know that show was your idea, kid," said Anushka. "All the good things that came outta last night are because of that big piece of Indiana cheddar you call a head. Ha!"

"We also know," said Rocco, "that you deferred higher education for the sake of the show. Frankly, I can't think of a bigger sacrifice."

"So we'd like to thank you for sticking around, m'lady," said JB, bowing grandly before her.

"We don't know what we'd do without you," said Tanya as the others nodded.

"I guess you can't deny that you're a part of something now," said Uncle Ross.

"I—I don't know what to say," said Corliss, who felt two things all of a sudden: that little hummingbird feeling in her chest and an irresistible urge to cry.

"If you don't know what to say, Corliss," said Uncle Ross. "Say you'll have a drink!" He left the room for a moment and returned with a tray of what looked like martinis.

"Uncle Ross . . ." said Corliss, shaking her head at him.

"Don't worry my dear, these are *'Bu*-tinis. A little seltzer, a little lime, and a little *quelque chose*, as the French folks say. Utterly wholesome and utterly a prime-time hit!"

Everyone grabbed a 'Bu-tini and raised their glasses.

"To *us!*" said Corliss. "Long may we reign!"

"To *us!*" shouted everyone.

Somewhere Near Someplace Near the Woods of Holly—Sometime Later That Day

The Bu-Hoo

And so, dear readers, it all ends happily—for now. The 'Bu-sters are back on top with their second week of boffo ratings, and everyone's all kissy-face with each other.

BLECH! WHO WANTS THAT????

I can't wait till they all turn on each other again, or at least get up to all kinds of hanky panky so I can report back to YOU. Because isn't bad behavior really what makes life worthwhile? Shady stars, drunken starlets, disorders, and addictions—me loves dat!

So stay tuned for more. 'Cause you KNOW I'll bring it!

Until that time, big 'Bu kisses and big 'Bu dreams . . .

'Bu-ternally ever after,
MBK